THE VIOLENT LAVENDER BEAST

THE VIOLENT LAVENDER BEAST

ERNEST HEKKANEN

THISTLEDOWN PRESS

Allen County Public Library
Ft. Wayne, Indiana

© Ernest Hekkanen, 1988

All rights reserved.

Canadian Cataloguing in Publication Data

Hekkanen, Ernest, 1947-
   The violent lavender beast
   1st ed.
ISBN 0-920633-45—5 (pbk.)

I. Title
PS8565.E45V5 1988   C813'.54   C88-098045-1
PR9199.3.H34V5 1988

Book design by A.M. Forrie
Cover drawing by Iris Hauser, based on a concept by Ernest Hekkanen
Photo credit: Lise Macleod
Typeset by Apex Graphics Ltd., Saskatoon
Printed and bound in Canada by
Hignell Printing Ltd., Winnipeg

Thistledown Press Ltd.
668 East Place
Saskatoon, Saskatchewan
S7J 2Z5

Acknowledgments

"The Wooden Arms of the Angel" appeared in *Wascana Review*, "The Violent Lavender Beast," appeared in *Canadian Fiction Magazine*, "Cadillacs and Chevies Don't Mix" first appeared in *Waves* and was later reprinted in *Second Impressions* (Oberon Press, 1981).

This book has been published with the assistance of the Canada Council and the Saskatchewan Arts Board.

CONTENTS

View Across the Meadow   7
When Death Comes Home to Roost   27
The Wooden Arms of the Angel   63
Moving the Patrone's Apple Tree   85
Cadillacs and Chevies Don't Mix   117
The Violent Lavender Beast   133

VIEW ACROSS THE MEADOW

On the ferry ride over to the island Leslie Gormant had spoken in glowing terms of everything they would do and see and experience, making the island sound as close to Paradise as possible without actually using that beleaguered word, although she had been pleased, and even ebullient, when her visitor for the week had replied that it sounded just like Paradise, for then it allowed her to say, no, she wouldn't go quite that far because, after all, the island did have certain drawbacks. There were only two grocery stores, one gas station, a thrift shop and a restaurant you had to phone in advance to find out if it would be open on a given day. But despite these inconveniences there were certain rustic qualities that endeared the island to her and, of course, the peace and quiet, and the pace, which was sublimely slow.

You got the feeling, as they sat on the vinyl-upholstered seats, heads nodding towards one another, that there was an element of intimacy, as though they composed a small island of their own there in the forward lounge, chatting quite animatedly, oblivious to looks which other passengers now and then gave them. Leslie was a sturdy woman of forty-eight, broad of forehead, with a shock of wavy, grey hair she kept trimmed fairly close to her head. Her eyebrows, by contrast, had remained unusually dark, giving her an intense, concentrated air when she looked at you with her pale blue eyes. She was the sort of woman whose bearing, and physical assurance, might lead you to think: there is someone who has spent time on a horse, although this would be rather far from the truth, as she had little experience of that nature. Her companion Stella Trulle was younger by at least six years, and was thinner, with a long, sloping face which tended in moments of solitude to become somewhat downcast and melancholy, as though worrying some small wound within her, and anyone could see her nails were bitten back, to the extent that it was painful to regard the fleshy, pink tips. But together, in conversation, the women seemed wonderfully whole, as though one's penchant for moodiness perfectly counterbalanced the other's liveliness, and vice versa.

They had, since boarding the ferry, completely lost track of time, so consumed were they by what they were chatting about, which almost entirely focused on the island and what Leslie hoped would be a unique and vital experience for her friend, especially as regarded the younger woman's writing. "Unlike in the city, where everyone pursues his own course, where there's so much chaotic activity, like so many billiard balls going off in contrary directions, there's a pulling together on the island—reliance on self but also reliance on others."

"For instance?"

"Well, for instance, there's no entertainment on the island. So what do people do when they want some, and believe me, there *is* want for some from time to time? Why they band together and create their own entertainment, be it a festival or a concert or a play. There's really quite an active play group on the island, with some pretty fine actors too, which surprises me. Yes, if I had the means I would retire over to the island right now. It makes my heart yearn every time I think of it."

Here, her visitor gave her a thoughtful expression. "So is it largely a retirement community?"

"Oh, no, far from it. Although how a lot of the people survive is beyond me. I mean, there isn't much commerce or anything like that. But somehow they do eke out a living. Why, there's even a school on the island."

"Perhaps you should apply?"

"Believe me, I would if there was an opening. But I hear there's quite a glut of teachers over there. Why that should be, I don't precisely know."

"Maybe they all have the same good sense," Stella said with gentle humour.

"Yes, now that might be," Leslie chortled. "We mustn't rule that out."

Leslie so wanted the younger woman to like the island as much as she herself did, she was afraid she was going on about it at too great a length, but for some reason she could not forbid herself this pleasure. There seemed a deep wellspring inside her from which details simply gushed, and Stella seemed content to sit and listen, at least from what Leslie could discern from the enthralled expression on Stella's face. Occasionally the younger woman would comb back her moderately long brown hair, as though out of some impatience, and Leslie would say: "Listen, I must be boring you, really I must," but her companion was always quick to contradict her on this point, and she would go on again, pursuing some tale about the island. She knew, in part, it was her own pleasure at getting back to her summer retreat that impelled her to go on in such a manner, as if, by degrees, she were committing an act of confession, to show where her heart truly lay. The ferry pulled in at Galiano Island and people seated around them got up in preparation for leaving, and then the ferry set off again, with deep, shuddering rumbles that came up through the steel hull, and before Leslie knew it the ship was making the hard-to-port turn that announced it was approaching its next destination.

"And now I really must stop," Leslie said, with slow, self-effacing laughter, "because this will be our stop."

"But there's been no announcement."

"It will come, shortly." She indicated the white channel marker on the rocky point. "Once the ferry has completed this turn you'll be able to see the terminal, set back in the landarms of the bay."

"These rocky cliffs which tumble down to the shore — I've been marvelling at them. They're so expressive, especially with all those arbutus trees clinging to the fissures."

"It is beautiful, isn't it?"

They had taken the evening ferry so by the time they drove to Leslie's place on the island, which was located as near the centre as one might get, it was only about an hour before darkness totally descended, and in that space of time Leslie wanted her friend to receive a good and lasting impression of the cabin and the surrounding acreage, one she could settle down with before nightfall enveloped everything. "I'm sorry it doesn't offer you a view of the beach," she said, as they climbed out of the Volvo station wagon. "But the beach is never far away, no matter which direction you take. A five-minute drive will get you practically anywhere on the island."

"Oh, it's lovely, Les. Lovely. And the cabin, it's so quaint."

The property was traversed by a hill that rose like the shaggy, humped back of a gigantic beast, and the small log cabin was situated at the foot, one side snuggled up close to an outcrop of rock so that on occasion raccoons would jump from the rock over to the foot of the house and she would hear them at night while she lay in bed. The front of the cabin actually faced the back of the property, overlooking a pond with a tumultuous fringe of grass growing around the perimeter. Not far from the cabin loomed an ancient arbutus tree, the bright, sinewy trunk of which seemed to contain an ethereal flame. A swing hung by two long nylon ropes from one of the branches, and immediately Stella ran over to it, sat herself down lithely and pushed off, thrusting her feet through the long grass as the swing brought her forward.

"Oh, it's grand, Les. I so envy you this place."

"I'm glad you like it."

"Oh, I do, I do."

The tall grass slapped against Leslie's pant legs as she strolled towards the swing. It had been a few weeks since she had last come over for a weekend retreat and she was amazed at how high the grass had grown, since she had cut it all back then with the lawnmower, from the cabin down to and around the pond, and further still, down among the fruit trees which grew along the barbed wire fence. From the adjacent property came the honking of a troop of white and mottled geese. They were advancing upon the fence, heads held high, looking off to one side at Leslie and Stella.

"They must think we're intruders," Stella said, pulling herself up from the swing and drawing close to Leslie.

"Whatever you do, don't cross the fence. Those geese are extremely protective. I once saw the gander chase the little girl up to the house. Screaming and crying she was, absolutely terror-stricken."

"Didn't her parents do anything?"

"Her father ran down to rescue her, and you should have seen the boot he gave that gander."

"You mean he kicked it?"

"Square on the breast. The poor thing actually flew backwards through the air, a jumble of wings."

"No wonder they're so mean."

"Yes, so whatever you do, avoid them. Avoid them like the plague."

Even as they stood chatting about the geese, dusk was filtering down upon them, as though it were a fine mist, a dampness that would gradually drench them. Leslie showed Stella around the property, acquainting her with the lay of it, how she owned up into the fir trees on the hill and as far back as the old logging road, now mostly overgrown by willow trees. There, by chance, they startled a deer, one which in turn startled them as it bounded for safety off into the bush, crashing with ungraceful force through the low branches of the willows. It took several moments for them to recover their former calm, as the start had sent blood pounding through their veins, raising a flush in their cheeks.

"I can see I'll have to get used to being surprised," Stella said, catching her breath.

"In the fall the deer come down to eat apples off the trees. I've actually seen them with their feet up on the trunks, stretching back their necks to reach the apples."

"Really? It must be wonderful to see."

"Oh, it is."

They entered the path that led through the blackberry vines back to where the outhouse stood amid the willows. Leslie had warned Stella about the outdoor facilities, and now, to dispel the uneasiness she felt on showing it to her friend, she related how one night her lamp had gone out enroute to the biffy and she hadn't been able to find her way in the dark, necessitating a premature stop. They laughed about it, then they walked on, down through a thicket of alders and across a plank spanning the width of a freshet, emerging into the fading sunlight and the orchard. Once again, the geese launched a furious honking, and for a few moments, overcome by the sight of their stark eyes, Stella simply stood watching them, lost in the act of peering. The large mottled one, which Leslie identified as the gander, kept snaking its head low through the grass, its beak agape, hissing. Where the two women stood among the fruit trees, they could see clearly up to the neighbour's light-green house on the knoll. No one seemed to be home, for no lights were on inside, and now, in the gathering dusk, lights would have been burning had anyone been present. At last, drawing Stella on with words to the effect that they should unpack the Volvo, Leslie led her towards the cabin, circling widely round the pond through the tall grass.

"Well, I know what I must do tomorrow," Leslie told her companion. "I must cut back this jungle before it gets any further out of hand."

"Is there anything I can do to help?"

"If you'd like to spell me on the mower, you're certainly welcome to. But it's not really necessary. I rather enjoy doing battle with the grass."

It struck Leslie, as they were strolling towards the cabin, that they had taken a wide, meandering loop around the property in order to end up there, nearly where they had begun when they had first gotten out of the station wagon. The cabin was a snug little affair. Having only two windows, a small one on the side and a larger one in front by the door, the interior gave the impression of being rather close and dark. Leslie referred to it as her den because, inevitably, on stepping across the threshold, she got the feeling that she was some great, woolly bear come home to hibernate. The cabin comprised a bedroom and kitchen-sitting area. Even with the electric light on the interior seemed dark and somber, owing to the rough logs which absorbed the feeble rays. Leslie drew back the curtains from the window above the sink, suddenly conscious of how shadow-laden the cabin was and not wanting it to adversely affect her friend, whose mood could swing very quickly, turning from gaiety to something dark and morose, almost as if a cloud had passed over her soul.

"It's really too small to live here all year round," Leslie offered, glancing over at Stella who was lifting back the curtain from the bedroom doorway in order to survey things back there. "But in a few years I hope to build a place up on the hill. The living room will have large, large windows, ones I can stand in front of so I can look down over the pond and the orchard."

"And what will you do with this place?"

Leslie shrugged. "I was thinking I might run a bed and breakfast. But who knows, I might simply use it for storage."

During the next few minutes they kept taking trips out to the station wagon, returning with great armloads of provisions which they scattered on the table, counter and floor. Leslie intended to stay the entire summer and had brought over a considerable number of effects. By the time they had put everything away, darkness had almost engulfed the outdoors. Leslie showed Stella how to prime the hand pump and then for the next few minutes they took turns pumping the handle, bringing up rust-coloured water that gradually began to clarify. When at last the water was suitably clear they filled a pot and put it on the stove to boil. Leslie lit the gas lamp and they repaired to the porch. There they set out patio chairs and a small table in preparation for tea. It was quite a large porch for the size of the cabin and during the summer, Leslie spent a great deal of time lounging on it, not much more than a lazy, slothful bear, or so she told Stella. A yellow hammock stretched between the posts which held up the roof and Stella found herself drawn to it, impelled to try it out.

"I used to love these things as a kid," she recalled, with a suddenly youthful smile.

"Be careful it doesn't flip you out."

"Oh, I know. They're dreadful for that, aren't they?"

And so they had tea, and for a long time, they said nothing, content simply to languish in the light of the lamp, taking in the night sounds: the croaking of the frogs, now and again the screech of a nighthawk, or, far off, the barking of sea lions. "I take it the beach can't be very far away if we can hear them this well," Stella said, referring to the jovial grunts and barks.

"I'd say a mile and a half. Then it would be, oh, another mile out to the island where they congregate."

"All that way, and still we can hear them?"

"It isn't quite like the city, is it? There sounds are muffled. Here they tend to carry. Like bells."

At that moment, a car went by on the road. Tail lights flared brightly through the dark of the trees, then up the way, towards the neighbour's house, there came the sound of closing car doors, followed by children's voices provoking one another and, immediately upon this, a man's voice harshly instructing them to "cut it out." Lights came on across the way, roughly tracing the progress of Leslie's neighbours through the house, then came the sound of a door, jarring open and jarring shut. Soon they saw a torch bouncing down through the dark of the meadow. The torch was met by honking from the geese, and this, in turn, was met by sharp yelps from a dog and quick, shrill whistles of a human variety.

"He must be locking them in for the night. Thank God, otherwise they'd be honking at the break of day."

The clamor died, and the torch travelled back up the slope towards the house, ultimately to be dowsed in the light of the back porch. They watched in silence, and then they heard, once more, the jarring of the door. The noise had killed the croaking of the frogs; however, they could still hear the jovial grunts of the sea lions, in the dark across the distant bay. "I think if not for the mosquitoes I could probably lie here all night," Stella remarked from the hammock, once the silence had become too wearing.

"Yes, they do tend to be a bit ravenous."

"Perhaps we should go inside."

"You know what, I was thinking that myself," Leslie said, swatting a mosquito on the back of her hand. But they sat a few minutes longer, neither wishing to make the first move to rise and go into the cabin. Finally Leslie, in her physically self-assured manner, put a seal on things by assembling the tea effects on the tray and taking them inside, and Stella, swinging herself out of the hammock and stretching lethargically, called after her, "What shall I do about the lamp, Les?"

Leslie was standing at the lighted kitchen window. She answered through the pane, "Smother it. There's a knob on the side. Just twist to the right."

The next morning they rose early, and for some little while, out on the porch, Stella sat with a sweater on, sipping at a mug of coffee while she worked on a poem. Leslie went for a trek up on the hill behind the cabin, ostensibly to locate the surveyor's stake at the northeast corner, thinking it would give her a better idea about how far up on the slope she could build. The bush up there was nearly impenetrable, so thick was the deadfall and the underbrush. After an hour of tramping about, crawling over trunks of rotting trees and shoving her way through salal, she came down again, into the warm sunshine, little more enlightened than when she had first gone up. She had suffered a pleasant pummelling in the woods, and she arrived back at the cabin feeling robust and fit. Immediately Stella glanced up at her from where she sat on the porch, and her eyes, so brown and deep, betrayed her alarm.

"Nothing," she said, smiling lamely, and Leslie could see when Stella fluttered her hands that her nails had been freshly bitten.

"You should have come with me. It was so invigorating climbing over all that deadfall, blazing a way up."

"Perhaps I should have. It seems to have done you a world of good."

They had a good, substantial breakfast of bacon and eggs, and afterwards Leslie hauled the power mower out of the tool-shed, which the tendrilous blackberry vines had nearly overgrown. With a plume of bluish smoke, she got the machine started and running decently, and then she began to assail the tall grass. Once in a while, in a really lush green patch, the engine would threaten to die, and once or twice actually did, when Leslie failed to pull it back quickly enough. Stella had remained inside to wash the dishes and she had yet to come outside. Now and then Leslie would glance towards the cabin, expecting to see her friend on the porch or in the dark doorway, unable to believe it was taking her so long to do the few plates and pans from breakfast. But then she would eject that thought from her mind and go on with the mowing, a job which was going to take her a lot longer than she had at first anticipated, the grass had become so lush and thick, particularly round the pond, where it came nearly to her knees. Gradually though, with hard resolve, she began to turn the tumultuous meadow back into something resembling a lawn. All the while a green scent billowed round her, so sweet and intoxicating it made her head spin ever so slightly, and once, in a sudden euphoric moment, she pondered throwing herself down on the cut stubble, rolling back and forth, trying to wrap herself in the fragrance. It was then, while she was in that slightly tipsy state, that the blade of the mower whirled with alarming, metal bites into some stones, and the engine stalled, quickly and decisively, with a sort of inner clank. Leslie wrenched the machine back out of the thick grass, and was about to restart it, when she heard high above her a sharp, piercing cry and, looking up, saw the eagles, three of them, gliding in wide, languorous arcs in the upper winds, one with a white head that glinted in the sunshine.

"Oh, Stella, come quick!" she shouted. "Eagles are circling above the hill."

She stood with her hand to her forehead, shading her eyes, slightly intoxicated by the green scent floating up around her, and yet mesmerized too, by the slow motion flight.

"Stella, you're going to miss them!" she hollered again, and there was a real urgency in her voice, a shrill desire. "They're so beautiful, so magnificent. Hurry!"

At last, Stella emerged from the dark confines of the cabin, her eyes wincing in the brilliant sunlight as she stepped down from the porch. Leslie watched to see if her visitor's face would register the sort of delight she herself had felt on spotting the eagles, and she wasn't disappointed, for all at once, a becalmed, awestruck look shone on the younger woman's long, sloping face, and her eyes, normally so dark and somber, beamed with bright intensity as she, too, shaded herself with an outstretched hand, looking up. Her hand was crooked in such a fashion her palm seemed to be holding a disc of sunlight, delicately but firmly round the edges.

"Oh, they're marvellous, aren't they?"

At that moment, the eagle with the white head wafted its large dark wings lazily, almost as if in slow motion, its movements veering it away from the other two. Its wings took the air with long, powerful strokes that seemed to curl beneath it, then it began to glide again, with ease and slow inevitability, gradually becoming smaller as it coursed down the fold between the hills, high above the reach of the fir trees. The other two, as though kept in tandem by an invisible yoke, responded with great, wafting surges of their wings, not together, but in counterpoint, and soon they were following after the first, well on the verge of disappearing after it down the glen.

"Such grandeur," Stella thrilled. "Are there many here in the islands?"

"A reasonable number. Nearly every time I come over I see one or two. But I've never heard them cry before. It was so high and plaintive. I was surprised. I expected something, well, throatier, I guess."

Suddenly a man's loud voice sailed across to them from the neighbouring house. It was a harsh, booming voice meant to bully whomever it was directed at, and Leslie found herself trying not to hear it. The man was yelling about someone having let the dog out of the house, and now she heard a woman's voice, too, high and strident, yelling at one of the children to get the dog back inside. The yelling was met by honking from the geese, down at the end of the property where Leslie knew there was a pond. She glanced over at Stella, noticing her friend's gaze was directed across the meadow at the light green house on the knoll. The shouting went on for several seconds, until apparently the dog was back inside.

"So how often does that go on?" Stella said in a low voice, directing a meaningful glance across the way.

"Fortunately not too often. He works in town so he's only here on weekends, thank God." She glanced at her wrist, only to remember she had left her watch on the porch, not wanting it harmed by the vibration and the yanking around of the lawnmower. "By the way, what time is it?"

"Almost eleven-thirty."

"I think I'll finish mowing this section down by the pond, then maybe we can have some tea and go for a walk to the beach. How does that sound to you?"

"Delicious."

Leslie pulled the cord to start the lawnmower. She yanked it several times, and each time the engine responded with a hollow, meaningless whirl. She tried a couple more times while Stella stood by the arbutus tree, her arms akimbo, watching with a concerned expression. "Could it be out of gas?"

"It shouldn't be," Leslie said, catching her breath, for she had pulled quite hard and strenuously at the cord. "I just filled it a little while ago."

Nonetheless she unscrewed the red gas cap and peered into the tank and, indeed, there was enough fuel, at least three-quarters of a tank. She checked to make certain the plug wire had not come loose, and she even applied a bit of spittle with one of her fingers. "A trick a friend once taught me," she said, smiling up at Stella, who had come over to help with the examination. She pulled the cord again, but the engine whirled uselessly, dead.

"I wonder if the gasline might be plugged," Stella offered.

"I wouldn't think so. It was working all right a minute ago."

"Could something have shaken loose, maybe a wire or something?"

They squatted beside the lawnmower, opposite one another, and very delicately they began to probe for things that might have been shaken loose. "There are a couple screws on this side," Stella said. "I wonder if they should be turned?"

Leslie leaned across the engine, so far across that their hair touched momentarily, electrically. Stella pointed at the smallish screws with Phillips heads, one of which was fitted with a spring. "They do look as if they should be turned, don't they?"

"Do we dare?"

"A little twist wouldn't hurt, I guess."

"I'll see if I can get my fingers on it." Stella made a pincer of her thumb and index finger. "Oh, yes, it turns quite easily."

"Well, give it just a bit of a turn."

"Maybe once around?"

"Yes, let's try that."

Stella gave a strained expression that indicated she was twisting the screw. "It gets harder as I turn it. Do you want to give it a try now?"

They stood up, Stella backing away from the machine, Leslie grasping the handle of the cord. She yanked the cord several times, without results. "Nuts. Something must be broken," she said, mopping her brow with the back of her hand. It was now a very warm day and she had hoped to get all of the grass mowed well down into the orchard. Between the heat and the mechanical failure, she felt an inner collapse, an extinguishing of her energy.

"Maybe we should try twisting the screw the other way?" Stella suggested.

"No, I think there's something seriously wrong. Let's just turn the screw back to where it was. I'll have to take the mower into town."

"Isn't there somebody on the island who can repair these sort of things?" Stella said, squatting beside the machine and setting the screw back to where it was.

"Not to my knowledge."

"Well, how about the guy next door?"

"I'd hate to ask him. He strikes me as such a surly bastard, pardon my expression."

"But they're the type who generally know about such things."

"Well, I know he does work on his car," Leslie said. "Last fall he was doing something to it and I could hear him swearing all the way over here."

"Well, it would save you the expense of going into town," Stella said, thoughtfully.

"Tell you what. Let's have tea first. I feel a little tired."

And so they had tea. Leslie felt sublimely mellow, not only because of the fine weather, but also because her summer break had come around at last, stretching before her as real and comforting as her island retreat. She would have preferred just to go on sitting there, surveying her property with calm detachment, fitting in and becoming part of the overall landscape, if not for the infernal machine, which she had left down in the field where it had stalled, prematurely putting a halt to her plans. That rankled her, for now she must have it repaired. Furthermore, Stella was probably correct. It was probably wiser to ask around locally for someone to do the repair rather than running off madly back to the mainland. She sighed, not wishing to think about it, any of it, simply wanting to sit there on *her* porch, on *her* patch of earth, soaking in the warming rays of the sun, allowing her gaze to wander aimlessly down past the pond and across the meadow toward the adjacent property.

They sat in silence, for a mood had settled over them, one that was tentative and quavering, until at last Leslie resigned herself to getting up and trudging down the road to speak to the man whose light green house could be seen quite clearly over the tops of the fruit trees. "I guess it would be presumptuous if I dragged the mower all the way over there," Leslie said, seeking, in a moment of worry and anxiety, Stella's counsel.

"I think I would inquire if he knew about engines. I think that would be the first thing to do."

"Yes, I guess that would be the best approach, all right."

Stella gave her a look of sympathy. "Would you like me to come with you? Two of us, together, might present a stronger force."

"Certainly. We could say we were out walking, when we thought we'd drop by."

Before they actually set out, Stella collected the tea things and took them back inside, and Leslie, fearing the sun's direct rays might cause the lawnmower's engine to explode, dragged the machine up into the shade of the giant arbutus tree; then, together, stride for stride, they headed out of the yard and down the road to the neighbour's. It was a brief walk, only a hundred feet or so, and it was no time at all before they had turned in at the gate. Along the roadway stood a windbreak of small fir trees and through the boughs, Leslie had spotted the man and woman doing something at a picnic table near the rear of the house. When they entered the front yard they were greeted by barking from a terrier that had its paws up on the window sill, yapping at them from inside. A young girl opened the door and stuck her blonde head out to peer at them and Leslie, as a sign of courtesy, asked if she might speak to the girl's parents.

"They're out back," said the small but sturdy girl. "I don't know if you want to go out back."

"Why do you say that?"

The little girl shrugged. "You can if you want," she giggled, as though at a private joke, rolling her eyes and acting giddy the way children in Leslie's classes often did, when they were called upon to answer questions in front of their friends. "I don't think you really want to, though."

"But why?"

"Cause they're doing animals, silly," and abruptly the girl slammed the door, leaving Stella and Leslie standing there in the front yard, staring at one another.

"Do we dare?" Leslie said, biting her lower lip. This, and the way she furrowed her brow, gave her an expression of heightened anxiety. She would much rather drop off the mower at a shop, and say simply, "It's broken, would you fix it please," and then pay the price, however much that might be. Her reluctance, combined with the little girl's warning, inclined her in favour of heading back out the gate.

"Well, we've come this far," Stella said, and on her long face was a look of urging. "It would seem rather silly not to ask. And besides, I'm curious, aren't you?"

"Well, yes, in a distant sort of way, I guess."

And so they started around the house. At that moment, the eagles flew back into view, only there were two now and neither had a white head. Leslie noticed them by accident, just happening to glance up. She pointed them out to Stella, and for a brief while they were stilled by them, in wonderful awe of the soaring and spiralling. Leslie felt a sort of tugging at her shoulders, a desire to spread her arms and glide, the same way children did when they imitated the flight of birds.

"Gorgeous," Stella said. "How I wish I could be up there with them."

"Yes, just think of the solitude."

It was her friend's momentum which finally drew Leslie on. She was still half-pondering the eagles when they came upon the couple, and what was going on, and the shock of it washed over her, nearly threatening to take her under. There was a high, almost sweet scent that her senses fought against. A tall, blonde woman was bent at the picnic table, and lying on the cutting board in front of her was the pink body of some small animal she was in the act of striking with a cleaver, hacking off the foot of what looked to be a rabbit. In two water-filled buckets beside the table were more bodies, stiff and soaking and flushed, while in the shade of the back porch, a freshly killed rabbit was hanging upside down by wires from a joist. There a dark-haired man in a T-shirt and jeans was undressing his kill, pulling the pelt in a single, sustained motion down to the shoulders. With a sort of subliminal awareness, he turned to regard Leslie and Stella, and at that moment, he let go the pelt, his rope-like arms hanging at his sides, his hands bloodied to the wrists. Leslie looked down and away, only to notice a blood-splattered chopping block, with a hammer lying on top. Beside that was a bucket of blood, and all around it were flies, and hornets, almost everywhere, buzzing, feeding on the scent.

The man was shorter than his wife, but very powerfully built, particularly in the shoulders, and he seemed perturbed to find Leslie and Stella standing there, not far from the table. The woman pushed her hair away with the back of her hand and gave them an embarrassed smile, as though uneasy about being caught in her present situation. Leslie felt too faint to speak when the man, in a voice that was not his own, for it seemed too suave, too gentle, asked what he could do for them. Leslie could not retrieve her voice, which had flown from her, nor could she let her gaze dwell upon him, especially his bloodied hands. She looked up and away, inadvertantly focusing upon the eagles. The man's gaze followed the trajectory of hers, and he gave a single, guttural utterance:

"Vultures."

"But we thought . . ." Stella stammered, finding herself short of breath. "You mean they aren't eagles?"

"Not those. You can tell by the tilt of the wings," and here the man gave a backward glance at the rabbit he had been skinning. "Look, we're kind of in the middle of things. Is there something we can do for you?"

Stella turned to Leslie, but Leslie, overcome by the smell and the heat, could not speak. And so Stella replied, "We came over, really, to ask you a question."

"A question?"

"Yes, we were wondering if possibly you knew anything about engines?"

And here, a smile edged across the man's lips, a smile not lacking in condescension. "Let me guess," he said, nodding across the low-lying meadow toward the log cabin. "Your lawnmower failed you, right?"

"How did you know?"

"We heard you hit the rocks," he said, shrugging, looking towards his wife who seemed to acknowledge and confirm the look. At that moment, the woman shooed a hornet away from the pink carcass. Then she grasped the carcass in one hand and slipped it into the water in the closest bucket, poking it down under the other bodies as if to conceal it.

"My name is Ann. I would offer you some coffee, but . . ."

"That's perfectly all right. We didn't come for coffee," Leslie said, at last, the volume of her voice startling even her, for she could not believe they were all standing there, so nonchalantly, with death all around them — on the table, hanging by wires, slicking the man's and the woman's hands, teeming in the very air. "Look, we're awfully sorry we intruded. It was most impolite of us." And then she turned to Stella, who had bent towards the table to examine whatever was in some stainless steel bowls. "Shall we go, Stella?"

But Stella seemed deaf to her. She was taking everything in with a show of curiosity, peering into the buckets, the bowls on the table. "So this is how it's done, is it?"

"This is how we do it," said the woman.

"You seem to have a lot of them here. Do you sell them locally?"

"On occasion. Some of these are spoken for."

"Someone once told me that rabbit meat tasted a lot like chicken. Is that really true?"

"It depends on what you feed them, but the meat does cook up white."

Now that the woman had taken hold of the conversation the man went back to the rabbit he had been skinning. Leslie, in spite of her disgust, found herself riveted. His strong, dextrous hands popped the forelegs out of the pelt, then he cut the pelt free from around the head and tossed it, inside-out, onto some others lying on a woodpile beneath the porch. Next, he cut off the head, slit open the belly and plunged the whole of his hand down inside, pulling out viscera. At that point, Leslie turned away, sickened and beside herself and, reeling slightly, began to leave.

"Leslie, are you going already?"

Leslie did not speak, could not speak. Her throat was constricted and she felt as though she might faint. She wanted only to get back to her retreat, away from the cloying fragrance of death, which she thought she might never cleanse her senses of again. Stella called her name once more, but Leslie did not answer, nor did she veer from her course, out through the gate and down the road, her pace quickening now, thinking how when she sat out on the porch of her cabin and looked off across the field, her view would be forever tainted, for across the way, there would be the light green house on the knoll, there to remind her of what she had just seen.

She turned in at her driveway and walked past the Volvo and, in her distracted and aimless state, she sought solace in the swing that hung from the giant arbutus tree, her vacant stare fixed on the small log cabin, or rather in its direction. She felt carved out inside, as though someone had reached into her and had relieved her of all desire, all life.

"Fallen," she muttered, as if to the heat, stirring her foot vaguely in the dust. Her rib cage lifted, it poised as though out of indecision and then there escaped from between her lips a sigh that seemed to empty her.

WHEN DEATH COMES HOME TO ROOST

Darvil Jenkins, now in that half-mad state just before waking, dreamed that a large prehistoric bird had flown in across the sea, inevitably to land on the foot of his bed. The creature gently fanned the air with its monstrous wings, now eclipsing the sun so Darvil lay in the shadow, now putting the sun in fiery view so he lay exposed and burning. Slobber was stringing from the bird's beak and its eyes were contemplating him in a vile manner that left Darvil with little doubt about its intentions. Again he was engulfed by shadow and blanched by light, in a slow, methodical fashion that made Darvil wonder if the bird were not trying to hypnotize him, then suddenly the damn thing pounced, and Darvil, fighting off what had sunk its talons into him, awoke to find he was wrestling with his mother.

"For crying out loud, Mom! It's your son, *Darvil*. Me, Darvil! Cut it out now," he said, not quite yelling, although his voice was loud enough to cause a violent tremor in the air. "Cut it out for chrissake!"

"Devil! Defiler!" his mother screeched back. "Caw, caw . . ." His mother, by far the smaller opponent, being a slight, knobby woman of sixty-nine, kicked and squirmed and squealed at the top of her lungs, like some wild, stricken animal. Darvil coiled an arm around her waist as he fought to free himself from the sheet that had tangled around his legs and crotch. At forty-one he weighed in at two hundred and thirty-seven pounds, most of it muscle that had turned into a gelatinous layer of flesh. But even though he was badly out of shape he feared as he grappled with her he might accidentally crush her ribs or break her arms because of her own thrashing around. With several exasperated moves he flipped Elsie May onto the mattress and very gently pinned her, just like he had done with so many youngsters his own age when he had wrestled in the one hundred and eighty pound class for Templeton High.

"Now cut it out, Mom! Before I haul off and bash you. Understand? Do you understand me?"

It was difficult to know, looking at her scrunched-up wren's face, with those perfectly black pinpoints encircled by washed-out blue, whether indeed she understood anything at all. To put it mildly, she had entered her dotage. She drifted in and out of knowing who she was and where she might be, an unfettered old woman aimlessly flapping off-kilter around the sun. At least it appeared that way on the surface, because sometimes she would really surprise him and her mind would function with the clear lucidity reminiscent of the librarian who had catalogued so many interesting bits of knowledge garnered over a lifetime of serious reading. On those occasions he would once again give up any notion he had of putting her in an old folk's home.

"There — are you gonna give up now — are you?" he said, firmly holding her down with a half-nelson while her bony breast bucked and heaved. With his free hand he combed the grey-to-white sprigs back from her eyes, and slowly shook his head. "You know, this has gotta stop, Mom. You can't keep goin' on acting like a crazy hoot. You gotta let yourself settle into this, just like Dr. Friar said."

Her nostrils were flared and her mouth, opening like a jagged knife hole, let out an ear-blistering screech . . . "CAW, CAW . . ." that he knew must have penetrated the walls of the house right out to the street. Lately her bouts of free association, as he chose to call them, had been getting a lot worse; she had become vindictive and quarrelsome, often biting the hand that kept her fed, until finally, yesterday afternoon, Millie had moved herself and the kids to a motel in town. What had sparked this was a little incident with a paring knife. Apparently his mother, seeming quite lucid and capable and "together", as Millie put it, had insisted on peeling and cutting some potatoes for supper. However, a few minutes into this task she had begun to giggle and snort in that peculiar way she had, as though her adenoids were choking off the expulsions of air. Then she started to stab the Idaho Gems, until they were systematically reduced to heaps of pulp. That was when Darvil had been phoned at the Freeway Auto Mart to come to the rescue. When he got home he found that Millie had had the kids lock themselves in the bathroom, with instructions to crawl out through the window and head for the nearest neighbour if they heard any screams or blows. Millie had armed herself with a broom, also with a cleaver she had stuck in the belt of her tight-fitting jeans. That and her sleeveless Flashdance pullover had made her look a wicked combination of street fighter and boy scout den mother.

"Now do you see what I have to put up with?" Millie had yelled, vaguely pointing the broom at Elsie May in the kitchen alcove. "See what you're subjecting me and the kids to—*that* over there!"

It wasn't very hard for Darvil to imagine Millie equipping herself with her weapons and standing poised in the hallway to the bathroom, her indictment ready to flow from her lips the moment he stepped through the door. He looked to where she was pointing the broom and saw his frail, grey-to-white-haired mother feebly stabbing at some mushy rust-coloured mounds on the formica table top. It was the methodical way she raised and lowered the knife that initially struck him, then the sardonic giggles that erupted from her throat. She was mumbling in an incoherent manner, like a little girl talking to her dolls, but her voice betrayed a quality that let him know the slushy piles were being chastised for some reason or another. Another little thing that caught his attention was the term of endearment she was using on the pulp. Once in a while, in between giggles and stabs, she would call the rusting mounds her darling little devils.

"Do you see now? *Can* you see now?" his wife was going on

in her half-hysterical voice, her eyes bright as fires in a face that could not be glanced upon by the sun without breaking into millions of liver-coloured spots. "This sort of thing happens on a daily basis, this madness or whatever you choose to call it, defecating in waste pails, lurching along the street bare-assed naked. She's dangerous, Darvil, and if you can't see that for yourself, well, you're *blind*—just plain blind!"

"I can see she's an aggravation to you," he said, reflecting on what she had told him over the phone, that his mother was wielding a butcher knife and would probably slit their throats by the time he got home, that is if he was inclined to come home to save them.

"Aggravation isn't the word for it. We are being harassed like this every day. Spat on and insulted, and it's got to stop."

Darvil held out his hands. "Well, what do you expect me to do?"

"Disarm her for starters. Take that knife away."

"Then what?"

"Then put her away, for chrissake! Where she belongs—in a home."

All the shouting between him and his wife, or rather all of Millie's shouting because he was trying to remain calm, had piqued his mother's attention enough for her to turn askew at the table and stare at them with what could only be construed as the innocently haggard face of a crone. And she had said, "My, but there's a lot of yelling in this house. It's enough to make a person want to pack up and move away," and dropping the paring knife in the rusting sludge, she very neatly rose from the table and sailed out of the room, blown by a breeze of indignation, with her aquiline nose held high.

"You see, she's done it again—on purpose," Millie fumed, tossing down the broom so it clattered on the linoleum floor and went slamming into the counter cupboards. "That useless old tit has done it again."

"Please, Millie," Darvil said, now raising his voice in order to be heard. "You're not being rational. If she's doing it on purpose then she can't be senile. You can't have it both ways."

"And neither can you. You can't have your mother and me, too."

"What do you mean by that?"

"I mean I'm booking out of this asylum — as of right now, this minute, and the kids are coming with me."

And that is what she had done; she packed suitcases for herself and the kids while Darvil stood by pleading for her to calm down and listen to sense. "No, if this situation makes sense to you then you're as nutzoid as your mother, and you deserve one another." Only when the suitcases were stuffed with every conceivable article of clothing, did she give permission to the kids to unlock the bathroom door and come out and then it was to whisk them towards the front door.

"Where are we going, Mom?" Now of kindergarten age, his son Ralph was a plump marshmallow of a kid, with leached-out blue eyes, reddish hair and freckles like his mother.

"We're going to spend the night at a motel," Millie explained, with an edge to her voice that was meant to cut Darvil to the quick. "Downtown."

"Is this the vacation Dad said we were going on?"

"It's beginning to look like it."

"But what about Pooh? I don't have Pooh with me."

Millie flicked her reddish hair out of her face. "Lindsy, would you run upstairs and get little Ralphie's Pooh Bear? Like a sweetheart?"

"Yes, Mommy."

Here Darvil twisted and seethed inside, not so much because he was faced with his wife and kids leaving him, no, rather because of the insistent way Millie had of making Ralph an ineffectual mother's boy. "For godsake," he said, "can't you stop calling him little Ralphie? You're gonna make him a fruitcake or something."

"Better a fruitcake than an unthinking brute," Millie blurted back.

Their raised voices had the effect of making statues of the kids. Ralph looked on the verge of crawling into a shell, either that or piddling in his pants. Lindsy, who had blonde curly hair like her Dad's, had screwed her face into a hateful, dishrag look that let Darvil know he was being scrutinized as if he were a bug. As usual on these occasions it was up to Darvil to demonstrate enough good grace to make a strategic withdrawal. "Do as your mother says, Lindsy. Get Pooh Bear—for Ralph."

"Should I, Mommy?"

"Yes, get Pooh Bear—for Ralphie," his wife said, her sort-of smile defying him to reply. Darvil could do nothing but acquiesce. However, he could not help but feel that by doing so his son was going to grow up with some sort of affliction he would bear with him throughout his life. He knew why it was being inflicted on the boy, too, and that was because of Millie and her overblown dislike of his mother Elsie May, whom she had never gotten along with, not from the moment they were first introduced. Millie had always been of the opinion that Elsie May, being a librarian and knowing a good many facts about a great many things, as well as how to spell so many obscure words in Scrabble, had always looked down on her. When Elsie May had sold them the house and surrounding acreage for a dollar some half-dozen years ago, with the stipulation that they let her live there rent-free for her remaining years—however long that might be, she had added with a smile—Millie had gotten her hackles up, saying in private that if his mother had really intended to do them a favour she would have let them sell the old place for whatever they could get out of it.

"Look," he had said at the time. "Where else are we gonna get a deal like this? You know what the economy's like."

"Yes, and I also know what it could be like if you only had a little more gumption."

All of these things had been going through his head as he stood there in the kitchen watching Millie drag Ralph by the arm to the door, with the largest of their suitcases pulling at her other hand. Darvil, more or less to demonstrate his good will, had picked up the other two suitcases, Ralph's and Lindsy's, and had toted them out to the station wagon and thrown them in the back for Millie.

"What motel are you gonna stay at?" he asked contritely, timid about raising her ire any more than it already was.

By now Millie had ensconced herself behind the steering wheel and was fumbling to light a cigarette as she instructed Ralph to buckle himself into the babyseat in back of her. That was another thing that irked him: being a fair blimp of a child, Ralph was far too big for the babyseat, but because he whined about having it taken out, presumably because he couldn't see well enough what was going by outside the car, Millie let him continue to use it, despite the fact that at his weight it would probably no longer prove a safety device if Millie ever got into an accident.

"That I haven't decided," Millie replied to his question about the motel. "But if you're worried about how much it's going to cost you . . ."

"I'm not worried about that."

"Yes, you are. You're always worried about how much *we're* going to cost *you*, so don't deny it. It's just one of your traits, being a skinflint."

"Oh, come on, Millie. I'm concerned is all."

"Baloney you are. If you were concerned about us you'd do something about your mother." At that moment her penciled-in eyebrow arced towards the sky and a cloud in the shape of a fist passed roughly across her face. "*Whom*, I might add, is watching us this very minute and probably giggling to herself in that stupid way of hers."

Darvil glanced at the second storey window directly below the gable. There he saw his mother, a shadowy figure in a darkened room, poking her head between the lace curtains, her index finger hanging from the corner of her mouth, now with a look of endless horizons in her eyes. "Don't worry, I'll figure something out," he said.

"That I *should* worry about," Millie said, "because every time you figure something out it always has a way of making things worse. Now would you please move your car so I can get out of here."

While Darvil was backing up the Trans Am and swinging it up alongside the aluminum garden shed, he saw Lindsy traipse out of the house and down the steps, gingerly swinging Ralph's yellow Pooh Bear at her side. Darvil got out of the car and walked around the Dodge station wagon to the driver's side. Lindsy had gotten in on the passenger's side and was passing Pooh back to

Ralph in the babyseat and Ralph was reaching for it in this horribly eager way that made Darvil want to barf, because he knew as soon as his son laid his hands on the bear his thumb would go straight into his mouth and his plump little fist would flatten his nose so it looked even more like a pig's. Darvil, by dint of sheer will, forced his eyes away from Ralph and found himself staring straight at Millie with the king-size cigarette in her mouth.

"I promise I'll get this worked out," he said.

Millie started the car, gunning it so hard dust flew up from under the chassis. "Fine, then do it—and don't get ahold of me until you do."

"But where are you going to be?"

"Find that out for yourself. After all, you're supposed to be the smart one around here."

At that, she slammed her foot down on the accelerator, swerving backwards down the gravel driveway in such an erratic, frenzied manner Darvil thought for sure she was going to end up in the ditch. Somehow she managed to miss the ditch and went swinging into the street, where, putting the Dodge into drive, she laid two streaks of rubber on the pavement in the direction of downtown.

Had Darvil not been consumed by so many thoughts he probably would have noticed his mother's mouth screwing around like a concrete mixer and would have been able to anticipate the spit that splattered with such horrible accuracy in his right eye. Darvil let go the half-nelson he was holding Elsie May down with and rose bullishly from the bed, gouging the offending mucus out of his eyesocket.

"Dammit, Mom. You're making it hard on me. You really are."

"Caw, caw . . . caw."

His mother, demonstrating a litheness uncommon to her age, rebounded from the bed and flew out of the room. A few seconds later he heard her feet scurrying up the stairs, then the slamming of her bedroom door. Darvil picked up a T-shirt from the floor and wiped his eyesocket and cheek. An immense feeling of helplessness came over him as he tried to sort out the mess that was now the beginning of another day. In his heart he wanted to complain: *Why me? What did I do to deserve all this?* except that he knew perfectly well the answer. He had screwed up; all his life he had spent screwing up and making bad decisions that ended up getting him into more hot water. He was what some people called an impulsive kind of guy. He threw himself into situations before he had fully analyzed them, as though to escape the anguish of logical deduction — he, who had shown such bright promise in his youth, with such an agile mind and quick responses. What had happened? He knew he was a smart guy. All of those I.Q. tests that had rated him at 130-plus were proof of it. So what the bloody hell had gone wrong? Why did he find himself doing the things he did?

Darvil threw down the T-shirt. He pulled on a pair of adobe-coloured slacks, scraped the coins and lighter off the nightstand and deposited them in his front pockets. He shoved his wallet into his back pocket, selected an undershirt from his dresser drawer and padded down the hallway to the kitchen where he automatically flicked on the T.V. before filling a pot with water and setting it on the stove to boil. The gestures came naturally since he was always the first one up in the morning. Millie had never been an early riser, although, during their first year of marriage, he had tried to insist she become one, only to find it less perilous to let her languish in bed an extra hour or two until her disposition had improved enough to approach her with a cup of coffee — a habit his mother had no little disgust for, claiming that if you let a bird lounge around in the nest too long you spoiled it for flight. He took a carton of eggs out of the refrigerator and began to plop them into a pot of water, reminding himself that he needn't put in any more than four because only his mother and he would be eating this morning. Then he plodded to the bathroom and got out his razor and Extra Foamy.

Last night around eleven o'clock, after he had polished off the Hill and Hill, he had come to the agonizing conclusion that he must put his mother in an old folk's home. This morning's little wrestling match had only served to confirm that it was the right decision to make; after all, if she was going to be attacking him, her only son, her only child, period, who else might she attack? Also, the dream he had had just prior to her flinging herself on him seemed to suggest it was the right thing to do. Obviously his sleeping mind had picked up her presence and had converted it into this prehistoric bird that was contemplating the best way to divest him of his flesh. She was preying upon him; the whole mess that she represented was preying upon him, giving him this nervous strain that was already beginning to build in his neck so that he could feel a slight headache coming on.

This obsession Elsie May had for mimicking birds actually went back a good many years. It first manifested itself back when she was going through menopause, at Christmas time not long after they had moved back into the house. Elsie May had become indignant over the seating arrangement and had risen from her chair, angrily proclaiming: "What am I — some little bird tossed this way and that by whatever wind happens to blow through this house? This is *my* home," she had said, her body stricken with sudden palsy that shook her greying thatch. "At least it *was* my home, until I gave it to you. That should at least guarantee me a permanent place at the table — one of my own choosing." Then, as if to demonstrate she was the little bird she had spoken of, she had flown out of the dining room, wafting her arms in this languorous manner that evoked a fount of mirth from Lindsy in her high chair.

Darvil rinsed the cream and stubble from his razor, contemplated a shower, but decided just to wash his face. His face, once so chiselled and hard, especially when he had been lifting weights, now seemed to bulge at the seams, not hideously, but enough to make him sensitive to how overweight he was. "Too much beer. Gotta lay off the beer," he told himself in the mirror. Instantly he recalled the previous afternoon, when he had just walked through the kitchen door to find his home in such an uproar. He hadn't told Millie, in fact he had never told anybody, but the term of endearment his mother had been using on the heaps of rusting potato pulp —"darling little devils"— was actually the source of his name. His mother had taken the first three letters of darling and the last three letters of devil and had linked them together in a chain that might as well have gone around his neck. She had explained this to him when he was going through the meanest throes of his pubescence, followed by a short description of how his father had run off to the Second World War to get himself permanently lost and presumably dead. Darvil had come to know his father by photographs only: a curly-headed young fop, dressed forever in army fatigues that seemed to disguise a certain tendency toward plumpness. And there was this devilish glint in his eyes, a smirking, sassy-assed look that seemed to laugh at Darvil's personal agony at the time. His mother, who had had a little too much sherry to drink that night, had thrown back her head and laughed almost hysterically. "And what a devil you've been to raise," she had told him. "I've paid, believe me I've paid for that night I let your father have his way with me."

Darvil was applying Wild Moss to his armpits when he heard the commercial come on T.V. He stepped through the bathroom doorway into the hall to catch it on the screen, which was angled so he could see it there on the kitchen counter. The guy from the local television station was on, Howard Mason, a mike in his hand, inviting all the folks in television land to come down to the Auto Mart to let Darvil put them into a deal.

"I hear you've really slashed your prices, Darvil?"

Howard Mason shoved the mike toward him, Darvil, whose hair was being tossed around by the breeze that inevitably came up at three o'clock in the afternoon. "That's right, Howard. We've got lots of fine bargains down here this week and, like always, our cars are guaranteed."

"Can you tell us about one of those bargains?" Mason said, shifting the mike like a gear lever.

"Yes, I can, Howard. I've got a Camaro down here at the Auto Mart that I'd like to own myself. It's a 1974, in mint condition, and all I'm asking for it is $3579."

Mason flicked the mike back toward his own mouth. "That's a great price, Darvil, I guess that's why you keep inviting folks to come down here to the Auto Mart."

"That's right, Howard. I've even gone so far as to make it my motto," and here the two of them, Mason and Darvil, pointed their index fingers at the folks in television land and jointly chimed, "Come on down and let Darvil put you into a deal. You deserve it."

Normally, at the end of the commercial, Darvil would have struck a glancing blow to the phantom chin of the public and would have shouted: "Attaway, boy. You tell 'em. You make 'em listen up," but this morning he couldn't seem to muster the proper enthusiasm. That great prehistoric bird seemed to be sitting on his chest pecking at his hide. As well, he knew in a few minutes he would have to phone Jenny Tiller. Phoning Jenny Tiller was something one had to work oneself up to because if anyone fit the image of a fish-wife it was she. A disagreeable woman from head to toe, with a stringy mop of brown hair she never seemed to wash, and crude, lumpy features that made you glad you weren't related, she always managed to make you feel pangs of guilt for wanting to hire her to do some "looking after". But it was Jenny, and only Jenny, who would consider "looking after" someone like his mother. Whenever he had hired her to spend the evening with Elsie May and the kids so Millie and he could go out together, say to a movie or a restaurant, they always returned home to be informed in graphic detail of Elsie May's misdemeanours: such as pooping in the wastebasket, which she did a couple times a week for some reason he could not fathom; or standing naked in the bathtub and hooting like an owl. Jenny's face always managed to let you know that you were imposing on her in some vast, probably cosmic, way but when it came time to grease her palm her hand was never held out in humility — no, she looked at the bills in her hand as if to snarl at them because there were so few, and so Darvil always ended up overpaying her.

Darvil pulled on his undershirt and trundled into the kitchen just in time for the water to start boiling on the stove. He popped a filter into the plastic gizmo sitting precariously on the pot, added coffee and began to pour water through. By now the eggs had begun to boil. He found two bowls in the cupboard and set them on the table where he noticed some potato pulp had dried to the formica. He fought down the image of his mother sitting there stabbing at the rusty mounds, shoved some bread into the toaster, poured some more water into the filter and called upstairs for his mother to come down for breakfast. There was no response so he called again. "Breakfast is almost on the table, Mom. Why don't you come down and eat with me?"

Still he heard nothing. No telltale creaking from overhead that would mean she was moving around in her room, no word spoken, absolutley nothing. The toast had popped up in the toaster. He took the butter out of the refrigerator, applied some to the toast, spread it around with a knife and tossed the slices onto plates. He poured the last of the water into the filter and, mumbling to himself about the stubborn-headedness of some people, he ascended the stairs to his mother's room. "You in there?" he said, knocking lightly on the door. "You ready to have breakfast now?"

He put his ear to the door; he thought he heard her rocking in her rocking chair, the rails of which he had taped foam rubber to because Millie had complained that the creaking back and forth was driving her nuts downstairs in the kitchen. Again he rapped lightly on the door, then slowly pushed it back. "Mom, breakfast is almost ready. You want to come down and eat with me before I go to work?"

There was Elsie May, stuck away in her oppressively darkened bedroom, rocking back and forth on the chair with her feet twined awkwardly through the rungs like some grown-up child. Her eyes were contemplating him in her ghastly deadpan way that made his skin crawl. It was obvious she hadn't heard him because her ears were smothered by the orange muffs of her Sony Walkman, which was no doubt turned up fullblast. It was hard for him to imagine that not so long ago she had struck quite a figure around town as a jogger. Indeed, an article had been done on her in the local newspaper, with a picture of her in her shorts and T-shirt, under a caption that read: No Average Granny in Sneakers. At that time she had been a specimen of good health, someone you'd look at and say, "That woman's going to live to be a hundred." But then her behaviour had begun to change. At first Darvil had chalked it up to an elderly woman's desire to indulge in a little tomfoolery, like the time they had found her out in the vegetable garden without a scrap of clothing on. But during the course of little more than a year this kind of behaviour had become rampant. She started to make anonymous phone calls to neighbours and to shoplift in the stores downtown. Dr. Friar, at first thinking it might be caused by something she wasn't getting in her diet, became convinced it was a sudden and massive onslaught of Alzheimer's Disease. "But she's always been such an intelligent woman," Darvil had told the doctor.

"Alzheimer's has nothing to do with a person's intelligence," said Friar, tapping a pencil to show that his time was being wasted by Darvil's concern. "It's a disease and it often runs in families."

Darvil bent over her and removed the orange headphones from his mother's ears and spoke solicitously to her. "Mom, I've got breakfast ready downstairs. Why don't you come down and eat?"

"I'd rather listen to Mahler."

"Mom, you've got to eat. You've got to have a good diet if you're gonna stay healthy."

"Mahler feeds my soul."

"Mahler-shmahler. Come down and eat before your eggs get cold."

His mother brought her chin up toward him and her eyes were so penetrating they seemed to skewer him. "My dear, dear Darvil," she said, slowly shaking her head. "My dear, dear, pitiful boy. You'll never understand, will you?"

"Understand what, Mom?"

But instead of replying, she just shook her head, back and forth, with this deadly serious look in her eyes. Darvil straightened up and backed towards the door. It was occasions like this one that made him doubt what Dr. Friar and everyone else was saying about his mother and her apparent senility. There was a mind behind those pinpoint pupils and sharp features and it was forcing him to communicate in ways he hadn't known before and if he was going to admit it to himself, it damn well scared him. What drove her? If she was alert, and thinking, what made her do these outrageous things like pouncing on him in bed, like frightening Millie and the kids? Darvil backed across the bedroom. He bumped into the door and glanced off to one side, clutching at the doorknob. He stared at his mother who was smiling darkly, her gaze slicing through him to the core. "Like I said, breakfast will be on the table. You can come down and eat whenever you're ready," he said and turned to go.

Precisely at ten o'clock, the hallway chimes rang and Darvil opened the door to find Jenny Tiller standing slump-shouldered and baggy-dressed on the stoop, her over-stuffed purse dangling from a bulging forearm. Battleaxe was the thought that came instantly to Darvil's mind each time he set eyes on her. A dark mustache sprouted above her upper lip and she weighed every bit as much as he did, he was sure. "Come in, come in," he said with the sort of enthusiasm he usually only employed down at the Auto Mart. "I'm sorry about the short notice, but something has come up."

"Has it really," she said, her voice plainly telling him she didn't believe a word he was saying. She lumbered into the room, depositing her massive purse on the table. "I thought as much yesterday when I saw your wife take off like a bat out of hell. In fact, I turned to Earl and I said pointblank, 'That was Millie who just went by. Millie and the kids. I bet something has happened over at the Jenkins'."

"Yes, well, that was very astute of you, Mrs. Tiller," Darvil found himself slipping into idioms picked up from his mother, and which he wouldn't be caught dead using on any customer down at the Auto Mart. But with Jenny Tiller he found it necessary to adopt a certain verbal distance. "Indeed, something has come up, something fairly urgent."

"Oh, and what?"

"Family matters," he responded, smiling. "Anyway my mother is upstairs. I attempted to get her to come down for breakfast, but I didn't have any luck. Perhaps you will. But right now I must be on my way. I'll call you up later this afternoon to see how things are going, and with any luck I won't have to bother you again like this."

"Finally putting her in a home, are you?" Jenny's large, lumpish face did nothing to disguise her contempt. "Well, I guess that's best. I guess that's how it's done nowadays. Not that I would ever want to be put away in one. No, siree. The things you hear about those places, why it's enough to frighten you."

Darvil knew at this point he was supposed to ask, oh, and what have you heard about them, Mrs. Tiller? But he was determined not to be lured into conversation with her. He knew she was one of those women he often found himself behind at the Safeway, one of those who inevitably had a *National Enquirer* stuck away in her shopping cart. "Yes, some of the things I've heard," she went on, dispensing wisdom like a vending machine. "The thieving and the abuse. Why I read only yesterday about this one operator — a woman she was too — who was taking gold right out of old people's teeth. But I guess it's like that around death," Jenny Tiller said, her smile a large crescent that folded into her rough-hewn cheeks, "every vulture in the woodwork comes out to roost."

Jenny Tiller, despite her clumsy mixed metaphors, was nonetheless expert at rousing a sense of guilt in him. She had been the one who had phoned Millie to inform her that Elsie May had been wandering around naked in the pea patch earlier in the summer, all the while claiming she wasn't trying to be nosy or anything, just neighbourly, adding that not every man was the sort of gentleman her Earl was. Apparently Earl had been out weeding in his own garden. When he had seen Elsie May parading around in the buff he had gone directly inside to report it to his wife. "But I guess it takes all kinds to make a world," Jenny now said in summation. "And I guess it keeps the rest of us from getting too bored."

"Yes, doesn't it," Darvil said, pulling on his sports jacket. His neck was becoming so stiff he wanted to pull and wrench at it. "As I said I'll phone you in the afternoon. Oh, yes, and feel free to make yourself some lunch. I think there's also a couple beers in the fridge."

"No, thanks, Mr. Jenkins. I never mix business and pleasure. It leads to bad habits."

"Well, suit yourself," Darvil said, glancing at his wristwatch. "Anyway, I must be going. I have a very busy day ahead of me."

Darvil shut the door and headed down the steps toward the orange Trans Am, consciously reining in his steps so it wouldn't look as though he were fleeing the site of a crime, as he knew Jenny would have her gaze stuck on his back. He folded himself into the seat behind the steering wheel, started the engine and glanced up at the window below the gable. He expected to see his mother's head poking out between the lace curtains, but, no, there was only a dark column. He twisted his head in a gesture that was becoming a nervous tic and his spine crackled down to a point between his shoulder blades, taking away a little of the pressure in his head. He backed the car out of the driveway and headed towards town. In the front yard adjacent to his own, he saw Earl in his train engineer's cap, running a push-mower across his lawn for what must have been the third time that week. Earl waved to him and Darvil, despite himself, waved back.

The Tillers' house was a low bungalow, unlike the Jenkins' large two-storey affair. At one time the area had been a farming community. Indeed, up the road, on the side of the creek, there was still some fenced pastureland, only rather than feeding milk cows, it now fed a horse belonging to the manager of the Commerce, where Darvil did all his banking. Darvil's house had been the farmhouse and was by far one of the oldest houses on Creek Road. It sat on three-quarters of an acre. He intended in the future to sell off part of it, that is once his mother died or was no longer mentally alert enough to know it was gone. The house his mother had slaved for in order to own outright had already been borrowed against to the hilt. Darvil had done it on the sly, telling neither Millie nor his mother what he was doing at the time, although Millie had grown inquisitive when she saw his name among the investors of the Downtown Redevelopment Group. Normally Darvil would have swung past the site to see how the construction was coming along prior to zipping over to the Auto Mart, but this morning he was running behind schedule and couldn't afford to waste time. When Millie found out he was one of the investors she managed to imply that that was why there was never any money for anything else. "Sure, you don't think anything of sinking money into some damn scheme. But when it comes to investing in your own family any deal is off before it begins." Once, in a virulent mood, she had threatened to tell his mother that the house was no longer theirs but rather the bank's, and lately Darvil had come to suspect that she had, in order to precipitate a falling-out between his mother and himself. The first hint he had of this was several months ago. Millie said she had taken Elsie May downtown to the library, apparently because his mother had expressed a nostalgic desire to visit with her colleagues who were still working there. "I don't think she saw your name on the sign, but I can't be sure," Millie had told him in the evening, with that edge of obstinate challenge in her voice that said: there, I've cooked your goose for you, what are you going to do about it? That was about the time his mother had taken her final turn for the worst. A few days later he had to bail her out of a shoplifting mess and for his trouble, she had called him a devil and a defiler to his face.

Darvil negotiated the cloverleaf that took him down the ramp onto the freeway and brought the Trans Am up to 70 mph. Five miles down the road he took the Aberdeen Exit past the Mac-Donalds and the Toys for Tots store and looped around to the Auto Mart. There he saw Gus, a lanky high school kid he had hired for the summer, scrubbing down cars that faced on the street. He waved to Gus as he got out of the car, called out good morning to the men in the garage and traipsed into the showroom where he kept a couple classic cars permanently on display. As soon as he stepped through the door Stella called to him. "There's a message on your desk. Millie wants you to phone her. She left a number where she can be reached."

"Thanks, Stel."

Oddly enough in the past few weeks, Stella was the only woman Darvil felt the least bit of harmony with; she was a year or two older than he, with a few grey strands beginning to show in her dark hair, which she always kept in a roll, not a tight-pulling roll that made a woman's face seem stretched and severe but rather a loose one that suggested it could come down at any moment. His face must have portrayed his misery because right away she cocked her head, looking up at him with this soulful expression in her dark eyes. "Troubles?" she inquired.

"My mother. Millie has come to her last straw with her."

"That's too bad."

"I guess I should have seen it coming," he said, and smiled. "Thanks for the message."

Darvil scooted off to his office. The telephone sat on the paper where Stella had scrawled: Evening Tide, 281-3674, Rm. 8. It irritated him that Millie had chosen to leave the message at the Auto Mart rather than phoning him directly at home. But obviously that was her intention: to create for him as much irritation and embarrassment as possible. He sat staring at the note several minutes before picking up the receiver and dialing. Millie did not answer in her room at the Evening Tide and Darvil told the motel clerk he would call again later. On his desk were a number of potential deals. One had to do with a guy who wanted to trade in a '79 Yamaha motorcycle, plus cash, for an '81 Toyota pickup. Both vehicles had about 45,000 miles on them, but the book price for the Yamaha, even if it was in excellent condition, which Darvil very much doubted, was only about a fifth of the Toyota, which had some problems with rust. The Toyota's windshield price was $5499 and this jerk with the motorcycle was trying to get it for a measly $1200. "God, what do people expect in this world?" he said, and wrote "No" in bold letters on the deal. "No less than $4300, with the bike."

Darvil buzzed Stella on the telephone. "Have you seen Al around this morning, Stel?"

"I see him out on the lot with a customer right now."

"Is it that jerk with the motorbike?"

"No, I don't think so. This is a family man."

"Look, that yellow Toyota pickup we've been advertising—you know the one. The bottom line on that is $4300 and that's with a reasonable trade-in. Okay?"

"I've got you."

"Good. I'm going to have to go out for a while—this family problem I'm having—I'll be back in a couple hours. Hold things down for me. We're running awfully tight this month."

"Will do."

"Thanks."

As he was putting down the receiver he realized how really upset he was with everything that was going wrong. His neck had stiffened up like some fossilized tree trunk and the pain was beginning to march up his spine towards his head. His neck was always where any strain hit him, the result of a wrestling injury he had suffered in the state finals, when his opponent had dumped him on his head in the only really humiliating defeat he had ever had. "Pinned me. Goddamn pinned me," he said, shoving back the plate glass door and crossing the parking lot to the Trans Am.

To get to the Evening Tide he had to backtrack along the freeway and take the Lacy Exit south. The freeway had forced the growth of the town to the north and even he would admit that that portion, composed of so many small businesses, all vying to make a buck, looked rather like a colourful, neon-lit shanty town compared to the older part of Templeton. The older downtown area was graced with the stately edifices of the courthouse and the post office, both of which were built of cut granite, back when craftsmanship still counted for something. Also there was the red brick library — Mom's library he had once called it — which had some fifty years previous been a railroad station. All these old buildings were gathered like elderly ladies around a memorial park endowed with frothy elms that splashed dense shadows over the streets. As a boy he had loved to pedal his bicycle downtown in order to recline in all that shade and stateliness, either that or to read in the musty confines of the library, which had been as much his home as had been the house on Creek Road. That had been back when he was still a bright hope in his mother's eyes, back before he had gotten tangled up with wrestling and cars in high school.

Some half-dozen years before, it was decided that the downtown area had become a financial drain on the rest of the community, and that's when the Redevelopment Group had been formed. The first proposal was to subject the library to the wrecker's ball since it was so over-sized and so under-used and cost the city a mint in maintainence and upkeep of the grounds. However, there was such an outcry from certain quarters, all those historical and special interest groups, of which his mother had been a member, the town began to explore ways of retaining the library as an artifact in the greater scheme for the mall, which was being designed in terms of an environment that would offer a sense of community (i.e., a swimming pool, a theatre), balanced out with revenue-making shops and restaurants and boutiques. Investors were offered the chance of getting in on the project and Darvil, hating to pass up what looked like an opportunity to strike it rich, had borrowed against everything he owned in order to get in on the ground floor.

Since it wasn't out of his way, Darvil decided to whip past the site. Never in his life had he had such a feeling of involvement as when he had decided to invest in the project. He went to all the Group meetings, threw his opinions into the fray along with everyone else's, hunkered down and fought for his point of view, alongside men much wealthier than he would probably ever be. Just to drive past the construction site where all the scaffolding was thrown up against the library's facade, where all those cranes and men and concrete mixers were pouring it on full steam, gave him a sense of exhilaration that usually kept him pumping at open throttle all day long.

Darvil pulled the Trans Am over to the curb and sat watching for a while, letting the activity on the site fill him with a robust determination. Even some of the stiffness in his neck dissipated, along with the knotted feeling in his jaws. Then he started up the car and drove the last few blocks to the Evening Tide Motel. He hauled himself out of the car and was heading towards the office when he saw Millie and the kids come waltzing down the sidewalk, each of them toting a shopping bag or box. Just eyeballing it, he would bet their stay downtown had cost him in the neighbourhood of a hundred bucks. By the end of the day it might be as much as two or three hundred, depending on how mad Millie wanted to make him. Darvil re-routed himself towards the sidewalk. When Millie and the kids saw him they visibly slowed their steps, the kids darting glances at their mother. "Hi there," he shouted, letting the salesman in him take over at the controls. "How was your big night out on the town?"

He held out his arms in a gesture that said: Come jump into

my embrace. He saw Lindsy take a couple of running steps toward him, before she came up short on the invisible chain linking her to Millie. Darvil, feeling foolish, dropped his arms. With slow, sauntering steps he walked over to Millie and the kids. "Well, what did you buy, gang?"

"I got a Star Wars outfit," Ralph said, hauling a box out of his paper sack, one with a cellophane window on the front. "See, Darth Vader. I'm gonna be just like him. Zap, zap, I got you," he said, pointing his ray-gun finger in the proximity of Darvil's crotch. Darvil winced; the very idea of his overweight son playing the role of the villainous Darth Vader was too much for him to entertain. But at least it was better than Pooh Bear.

"How about you, Lindsy? What did you get?'

Lindsy was at that awkward age approaching puberty. She was constantly flip-flopping between being a little girl in pinafores and a grown-up girl trying on makeup. "Clothes," she said, hideously screwing up her face.

"Well, what kind?"

"Just clothes," she said, with that snotty tone that nearly drove Darvil to violence; it made him want to take her by the shoulders and shake her roughly. After all, where did she think the money came from for those clothes? His pocket, his sweat. Instead he smiled vaguely and said, "Well, I guess I should have known that."

He had been intentionally avoiding Millie's gaze. Now he looked at her. Her face had become puffy from the monthly edema that had set in and her eyes were as hard as blue ball bearings. The large sack she gripped at her wrist was nondescript but probably contained fabric and patterns. Her sewing room, which had once been his study, was crammed full of projects started and put aside. "I got your message," he said. "Thanks for leaving it at the lot."

"You're welcome," she said, her smile the nearest thing to a mannequin's. "I didn't want you to ignore it."

"As you can see, I didn't," he said, offering a laugh. The dreadful pain was marching up his spine again, his temples beginning to throb like engines.

Ralph tugged at Millie's arm. "Mom, I want to go try on my Darth Vader—come on."

Millie struggled with her purse. "Here's the key to our room, Lindsy. You go open up. You can take my bag, too."

"Gee, do I have to?"

"Yes, now go."

Lindsy made a face but took the keys; she and Ralph straggled off across the parking lot to the Evening Tide. "Well, what have you decided?" Millie said. The sunlight on her face brought out the paste under her freckles, making the latter look as if they were decals strewn by the wind across her features.

"What do you think I've decided? I'm going to put her in a home, of course. I have no alternative."

"Where is she right now?"

"Jenny's looking after her. By the way, Jenny saw you drive off with the kids yesterday. I imagine it's all over town by now, something to the effect that you've left me."

"I didn't *leave* you. I only suspended communications."

"Well, whatever. I'm sure Jenny has got the word out."

Millie dug around in her purse. "I thought you might come to your senses so I took the liberty of phoning around to some homes." Here, she pulled a crumpled paper out of her purse and tried to smooth it. "These were the places that seemed fairly reasonable."

Darvil took the wrinkled note paper. From the crumpled and frayed appearance he figured the paper had been in her handbag for at least several weeks. Quite probably she had been waiting for his mother to do something that would let her rush off to the motel, with the kids in tow. He noted the monthly fees penned in across from each home, places with names like Langara Leisure Home, The Shady Rest, Twilight Time Estates and Autumn Years Ranchero. "God, these places are a fortune. Where am I going to come up with five to six hundred bucks a month?"

"Your mother's pension will pay for most of it."

Darvil cracked his neck. "Do you know what she called me this morning? She called me her poor, pitiful boy. And you know what? I'm beginning to think she's right."

"What's the matter? Are you feeling sorry for yourself again?"

"No, but I very definitely feel as though I'm in a cross-fire."

"Well, if you don't want to put her in a home it's up to you. It's your decision. But you'll have to find another place for me and the children."

"No, I'm putting her in a home. Rest assured of that."

"Then stop complaining about the cost, and get started. The sooner this is all over the sooner you'll have us back. That is, if you want us back?"

"You know I do, Millie."

"Good, then it's all settled," she said, walking past him towards the Evening Tide, as the elm leaves rattled overhead. Abruptly she turned and smiled. "Oh, by the way, we'll be dining at the Las Tapas tonight. Feel free to join us. We'll be eating around seven, I think."

"Thanks," he said flatly.

"You're welcome," she said and, swishing about pertly, headed into the motel.

The next couple of hours Darvil spent travelling from rest home to rest home. His neck was now so stiff it felt almost immobile, his jaws ached at the hinges and the pain that originated in his spine had surged right up into his skull, where tracer bullets were flying around, lodging in tissue here and there with deadly little smacks. As he suspected, the list of rest homes was stale. He found that out at the first place he tried, The Langara Leisure Home, where he was rather rudely informed that there were no vacancies, in addition to which it was proper to first make an appointment. After that rebuff he spent a few dollars on candy bars at a corner store in order to come up with enough change to phone around to the various places. Those that required appointments he relegated to the bottom of the list and those he could visit immediately he put at the top and once again he headed out in the Trans Am. By one o'clock he had visited no fewer than six homes and was amazed to find that there were so many old people in need of care in Templeton. Finally he had narrowed down his choice to either Twilight Time Estate or Autumn Years Ranchero.

The woman who ran the Twilight Time—she was sixty if she was a day—had recognized him as "that guy on those car commercials." A chipper, wry person, with awesomely thick-lensed glasses that she was always pushing up on her nose, she did most of the talking while Darvil did nearly all the listening. She showed him around the facilities, which were located in a large, rambling house with columns in front, and everywhere she went she stopped to chat or say hello to the elderly inmates. "I *do* think of them as inmates," she had told him quite frankly. "They aren't here under duress or anything, but let's face it—they *are* living out a sentence. Depending on their health, etcetera, the term is either longer or shorter, and I see it as my duty to make it as pleasant as possible. We have games, get-togethers, special events, and there's a television in every room."

The Autumn Years Ranchero was located on a couple of rolling acres that could have substituted quite nicely for a golf course. It offered individual housing units for couples able to look after themselves, right up to full care facilities for enfeebled or senile patients, but the director, a man by the name of Dr. Emberly, had none of the warmth or charm that Adele Price had at the Twilight. Emberly had also recognized him from the commercials and, in a stab at winning Darvil's favor, had said that he was looking for a car, something along the lines of a Mustang or Valiant, for his daughter's birthday. The doctor had whisked him around the Ranchero in one of those motorized golf carts, pointing out the advantages his mother would have living at the institution. But everywhere Darvil looked he saw old people staring out of doorways and windows, with a common, accusing glare in their eyes, rather like the bovine stare of cows let out to pasture. The old people at the other homes had the same look in their eyes, one that was aimless and wandering, but it hadn't been coupled quite so closely with the impression that the patients were livestock on a ranch. He could figure no other reason for calling the place a ranchero, because there weren't any animals or anything, and this in the end was what inclined him in favour of Twilight Time.

Having made what he thought was a rational, well-thought-out decision, he drove back to the Auto Mart where he intended to phone up Adele Price to inform her of his intentions. However, the moment he stepped in through the showroom door he was waylaid by Stella, who informed him some woman by the name of Jenny Tiller had been trying to get him for the past hour or so. "She seems to think it's fairly urgent, but she wouldn't say what it was."

"Good God, it must be about my mother."

Darvil went directly to his office to place the call. Jenny's gruff voice conjured up an image of that great, stolid woman, unsettled by having fallen on a banana peel or something equally slippery. "I'm glad you finally got ahold of me, Mr. Jenkins," she said in her accusatory manner.

"Well, what is it, Jenny?"

"Your mother—she's plain up and disppeared. Vanished."

Darvil closed his eyes momentarily, trying to calm himself. The throbbing in his head intensified, the bullets went zinging. "What do you mean, she's disappeared?"

"Just that. I can't find her anywhere."

"Well, when did you last see her?"

"At lunch. We were sitting down here in the kitchen—we were having some nice Campbell's chicken noodle soup—and suddenly she got all huffy and went upstairs. There's only one way down from up there, so I thought, well, I'll just sit myself down in the kitchen and read a little of my book. But after a couple of hours or so I got suspicious because I wasn't hearing not even a sound. I went up to look—and, well, she was gone. I couldn't find her anywhere."

Darvil sighed. "Have you checked under the beds? Sometimes she'll hide under someone's bed."

"No, I didn't think of that, Mr. Jenkins."

"Well, please do so. By the time you get done with that I should be home. I know a place in the basement where she hides now and then."

Darvil slammed the receiver, hoping the noise would penetrate to the pit of Jenny's thick brain. He found the Tylenol in his desk drawer, gobbled down four of the tablets with the aid of some black coffee and told Stella he would have to desert the fort again.

"Apparently my mother's on the loose. Anyway the babysitter can't find her."

"Ah, that's too bad. I really feel for you."

By the time Darvil got to the house his headache had made him quite nauseous. He barely climbed out of the car when his stomach began to lurch; he bent over, holding himself up against the bright orange fender, and retched into the dust of the driveway. Once, then twice, then a third time, the thick fluid beading onto the ground at his feet. Darvil yanked at his tie, wadding it up and throwing it back into the hot confines of the car. The sunshine was suddenly so bright he thought he might faint and he knew Jenny, if she had seen him throw up, would automatically assume he had been drinking; indeed, as he turned away from the car he saw her at the door, holding back the screen.

"What's the matter, Mr. Jenkins? Are you feeling poorly?"

Darvil hitched up his trousers and headed for the door, unprepared to take any guff from Jenny. "No, one of my headaches," he said, rubbing his forehead and squinting at her through the bright, spangling sunlight.

"You should have yourself checked out."

"I don't have time for that, Jenny. Have you found my mother yet?"

Darvil pushed past her into the dark living room, knowing from the way she was behaving what the answer would be. "I checked under the beds like you said. Nothing. Absolutely nothing."

Darvil went into the kitchen, hollering for his mother.

"I don't think you'll get her to come like that, Mr. Jenkins. I've tried already."

On the kitchen table, as if to prove what she had told him over the phone was true, he saw a book turned pages-down on the formica, one of those romance novels by Violet Somebody. Also, he saw a bottle of beer and a small glass. "I thought you said you never mixed business and pleasure," he said, his headache easing somewhat now that he was in the shade and cool of the house.

"Look, I'm not going to hide anything from you, Mr. Jenkins. The house was so hot and stuffy, and I was so dehydrated, I thought I'd have a little sip from one of those beers you said was in the fridge. You can see yourself there's only a little gone in the bottle, just enough to cool myself off."

Darvil opened the door to the basement and headed down into the dark, thinking his mother might have sneaked past Jenny and gone down to the furnace room, where he had found her a couple of times, hiding in the cubby hole under the twisted conduits of the hot-air vents. Just as he flicked on the light, he heard the phone ring and Jenny's voice calling him to come up. "I think they've found her, Mr. Jenkins."

"Who's found her?" he said, turning and bounding up the stairs. Jenny did not reply. When he turned the corner into the kitchen he saw her holding out the phone, with her hand clutched to the mouthpiece, her lower lip clamped between her teeth. "She's downtown, Mr. Jenkins."

"Downtown! How the hell did she get down there?" Darvil roughly grabbed the receiver out of Jenny's hands. "Hello, this is Darvil Jenkins. Who am I speaking to?"

"This is Louise Ingstrom down at the library. We have a bit of a problem down here."

"So I hear. I'll be right down to get her."

"Well, it's not going to be quite that simple. You see, the fire department is here . . ."

"Oh, god, no. Don't tell me she's set a fire."

"No, not that. You see, she's up on the side of the building . . ."

"The side of the building! How did she get there, for crying out loud?"

"Well, it looks as if she just walked right up. Anyway, she refuses to be helped down, so I'm calling you."

"I'm glad you did. I just got word she'd flown the coop." he said, skewering Jenny Tiller with the most loathsome look he could give her. "I'll be right down. Five minutes at the most." Darvil hung up the receiver. "What in the hell did you say to her anyway?" he told Jenny.

"Nothing. We were just talking over lunch. Going on about things."

"Like what?"

"Well, she was wondering where everyone was."

"So you told her—in every gory detail, I bet."

"Now, Mr. Jenkins, it wasn't quite like that. I might have said something about a rest home, but it was only to test her feelings. It was a question, is all. How she felt about such things."

"Thanks, Jenny. You were very helpful." He dashed off the Evening Tide's phone number on the back of one of his business cards. "That's where my wife is staying. Get ahold of her and tell her what has happened, and try not to fail this time."

Darvil ran out to the car and swung it around in the direction of downtown.

The first thing he noticed when he got there was the absence of any noise. The usual afternoon wind had come up and was flinging dust through the memorial park, where the grit zinged against the heavy foliage of the elm trees, but except for that everything was still. Parked in front of the library was a fire truck, an ambulance and two police cars. As well, a crowd was gathering back under the trees. Darvil put his hand to his forehead and scanned the scaffolding in front of the library for his mother. The wind carried the smell of cement, a smell surprisingly sweet and yet acrid. Dust beat a tattoo against his face, some of it lodging in the corners of his eyes. His first once-over glance of the facade revealed nothing of his mother; indeed, he found himself rather distracted, unable to make sense of the erector-set mishmash of girders, cranes and reinforcing bars that seemed to poke like porcupine quills from all over the site. Men and machinery had come to a halt, suspended in awkward, uneasy poses as though awaiting someone to trip a switch that would turn them back on, this while the dust sailed through the air, partly obscuring the blue sky.

It was almost by accident that he spotted his mother. She was tucked away in between some low-standing columns just under the first new floor of construction, which in the new plan for the mall would become no more than a formidable guard rail along an open-air promenade. She had wedged herself between two columns, having either lowered herself down from the scaffolding above or having scaled up from below. How the hell she had made it up there without being restrained or at least noticed was totally beyond him. Certainly an old woman in orange shorts and a T-shirt, one who was partly out of her mind, careening randomly off the world like some madly driven cue ball, would have called enough attention to herself for somebody to have stopped her. All one of those surly workmen would have to say was something like: "Hey, lady, what are you doing up here? Get your skinny old ass back down on the ground where it belongs." But, no, there she was, now flapping one arm while she clutched a column with the other.

"Damn her senile hide," Darvil mumbled, heading up the granite steps to the main entrance of the library. A policeman reached out his hand to detain Darvil, a gesture that came off like a priest conferring benediction. "It's all right, officer," Darvil told him. "That's my mother up there. I've come to retrieve her."

"You're Darvil Jenkins?"

"That's right."

Inside, the library revealed none of the chaos of construction. It seemed a sanctuary, a place totally unconfused, untouched, pleasantly cool and silent, books properly arranged on their shelves, the proper musty odor of scholarship all around. Over at the counter the chief librarian nodded at him as he came through the door and the policeman she had been talking to turned to glance at him prior to walking over. Again he was asked if he was Darvil Jenkins, a question that was beginning to irritate him, although he knew it had to be asked.

"That's right, officer. I see my mother has brought things to a halt down here."

The officer was about Darvil's age. However, in uniform, with a weary I've-seen-it-all look in his eyes, he managed to look older. "That's what she wanted—all the noise to stop."

"I see."

"Shall we go?"

"I'm ready if you are. I don't want to keep things shut down any longer than necessary."

They rode the ancient elevator to the third floor. It was an ornate throw-back to another era when elevators were endowed with scrollwork and ascended to their destinations with the direction of Millie's voice, past a flurry of absurdly waving hands. He felt his back slam into something hard, then he found himself thinking of that great prehistoric bird he had dreamed of so long ago that morning, the one that had exposed him alternately to the light and the dark — this, while he tumbled head over heels into what seemed an all-consuming vastness.

THE WOODEN ARMS OF THE ANGEL

Ethel Rimley, who at the moment was dressed in a crocheted bedspread she adamantly referred to as her toga, stood at the side door to what had once been the garage before her husband Ken had turned it into his darned old carving shed and tried to make out what he was saying and to whom. She knew if she tried to twist the doorknob she would find it locked, a measure he had taken to guard against her sudden intrusions, which he maintained always put such a damper on his creativity. She could hear his voice plain as day, but he was speaking in some kind of slang language she could not completely understand; she didn't know exactly where he had come by this talk but she knew roughly when he had started to use it, about a year ago when he turned his motorscooter in for a Harley-Davidson and started wearing all those godawful black leather duds. In her book, there was nothing more ridiculous than a sixty-seven year old man riding around acting like a young jack with plenty of milkweed in his jeans.

Until his retirement Ken had been so mild-mannered she might have called him lacklustre. For thirty-four years he had been a custodian with the local school district and in all those years there hadn't been so much as a blemish on his record. He had always brought home his pay cheque intact and he had always been careful to pay off the mortgage. If ever he had a vice it was his carving, but even that had not been too hard to overlook in a man as perfect as her Ken, at least as long as he had stuck to practical things such as back scratchers and book ends and table lamps. Ever since she had known him shortly after he got out of the navy he had been whittling on some piece of wood. At first she figured it was nerves; some people smoked, some people fidgetted, but her Ken, well, he carved. Give him a block of wood to sink his blade into and you couldn't find a happier man on God's green earth.

Once there was a time when she had gone out of her way to brag about his carving because it was a hobby that kept him at home. But when he got older, around fifty-five or so, he started taking his whittling to heart, entering his sculptures in fairs and shows, and each time he sold a piece he became more serious and spent even more hours out in his shed, until now, she hardly saw him at all except at meals and bedtime, at least until he got himself that damned Harley-Davidson. Now she saw him so rarely it was as if they weren't even married any more. The trouble was, he had made such a go of his carving, selling pieces for as much as several thousand dollars a whack, he thought he was some sort of Picasso who could do just about anything he pleased.

But to her he was still plain old Ken, her husband of over thirty-five years. Most of that time had been as close to bliss as you could come. Sure, they had had their fair share of squabbles, that was only natural, but because they had once done things together, like bowling and playing bingo and going to church on Sundays, they had managed to stick it out together. They had never had any children, which she had chalked up to some war-provoked trauma that had made Ken impotent. At least she had figured this to be the case until last week when this scraggly, blonde-haired girl had showed up at the front door, her belly bulging between the flaps of a black leather jacket, hardly covered up at all by the pink T-shirt with the thick black arrow pointing directly at her now prominent belly button, over top of which some black lettering declared: *Another Biker's Brewing.*

"Is this where Kenny lives?" she had said, flicking her head about so her oily hair flipped over her shoulder. Obviously she had arrived by motorcycle. There were three of the big black and chrome things parked at the curb behind her blue Maverick, cocked over to one side, looking so nasty Ethel succumbed to a frightful tremor. There was a woman standing beside one bike, her arms akimbo, with brunette hair hanging halfway to her bottom and what looked like a tattoo on her left cheek. A guy with a beard was sitting side-saddle on another bike, wearing these mirror-like sunglasses and grinning like some ape. Even from the distance of the house Ethel was certain she could see that his mouth was full of decayed teeth.

"What do you want to know for?" she had replied to the girl, for even Ethel could see, under the snarling, rough exterior, she was no more than twenty-three at the very most.

"Look, I don't want any static, lady. I'm just asking you if this here is Kenny's digs?"

"My husband Kenneth lives here if that's what you're asking me."

The girl smiled and by God, she had dimples; they even made her look cute. "Well, you tell Kenny I decided on a name. I'm gonna call it Rip if it's a boy and Angel if it's a girl."

Ethel's jaw had threatened to fall out and clank on the stoop, but she managed to firm it up enough to seem under control. "My dear, I don't know what you're talking about."

The girl placed her hands on either side of her huge belly, as though offering it to Ethel. "I'm talking about this, what's in here."

"Well, I'm sorry," Ethel told her. "But it can't be my Ken's because my Ken," here Ethel strove for a good likeness, instantly finding one in the red hose that snaked across the lawn to the sprinkler, which had been arcing spray ever since nine that morning, "my Ken's as impotent as a garden hose."

"Well, he sure did a hose job on me, that's for sure. So you tell him, huh? Tell him if he doesn't own up Shirley's gonna muscle him."

Then, with a wink, Shirley skipped down from the stoop and walked straight off across the lawn through the drenching spray of the sprinkler, laughing hilariously to her friends. The three of them kick-started their bikes, the noise rumbling like thunder coming in over the hills, and they tore off at breakneck speed down the quiet suburban street. Ethel had walked around in a daze nearly all the rest of the afternoon. Had Shirley and her friends not been wearing the same sort of black leather duds her Ken wore, and had they not been riding those same machines that looked as if they were going to cart their riders straight off to hell and beyond, she would have dismissed the episode as a case of mistaken identity. Surely the Shirley who came to the door couldn't be looking for the Kenny that was her Ken. It all seemed to be such a bad dream. She poured herself a cup of lukewarm coffee and sat down at the table in the kitchen alcove. Fifteen minutes later, she hadn't so much as glanced at her coffee cup. Her eyes wouldn't seem to focus. All they did was take in the flecked brown and swirling gold of the formica table top.

"Maybe I should pinch myself to see if I'm dreaming," she said, looking down at her pudgy hands which were purple and quite cold for such a warm afternoon. She dug her fingernails into her flesh and squeezed; she squeezed hard until there was quite an indentation in her skin and decided that she wasn't dreaming after all, just numb to the point of feeling dead. She looked out the window at the garage which was now Ken's studio, knowing he was inside whacking away on what he had come to call his masterpiece. He had had the mammoth block of imported teak all aged and cured and dehumidified, which she figured must have cost him a small fortune. It was lifted down by a crane from a flatbed truck and rolled on a trolley into the garage where Ken had shut the door on it about five months ago. She remembered the boyish look on his face when he told her his next project would be the one that would probably make him immortal, if only he could do it right. The idea of her Ken becoming immortal because of something he was about to whittle out of wood was just too much for her to entertain and she had said, snatching up his dinner plate and trotting it over to the kitchen sink, "I think I liked it better when you did table lamps. At least you can read by a lamp, or crochet."

"Yeah, but Ethel, anyone can do a frigging lamp. No one's gonna remember you for it either, not once the light goes out. They're just gonna bitch about having to get a new bulb."

Whatever kind of logic that was she did not share or sympathize with it. All his grasping for immortality meant to her was that he would spend just that much more time out in his darned old carving shed. Sometimes he never even came to bed. She figured he must have a cot out there that he used on nights when he was really possessed. However, she didn't know for sure; he hadn't let her into his studio for over three years, because of a comment she had made about a carving he had done of a boy riding on this godawful snorting pig with tusks. Her exact words were, "Who in his right mind is gonna buy that ugly hunk of wood? People like things that are pleasant, Ken. A pig isn't pleasant. It's ugly and mean-spirited. And besides, why should that boy be smiling? I wouldn't find it any fun riding a pig, not likely."

But just the same he had sold the piece for something like six thousand dollars, the biggest sale he had ever made. That, he maintained, had vindicated him, while she maintained that it only proved how crazy some people really were, at which he waved his hand, as though sweeping her and her opinions under the rug, and headed back out to the garage, leaving behind him a trail of wood chips on the linoleum and the carpet.

At five o'clock, Ken would put the receiver back on his field telephone so Ethel could ring him up from the field telephone in the house to see whether he was going to come in for dinner. Ethel was in such a trance because of the pregnant biker who had come to the door, she just sat and watched the minute hand trip past the twelve and systematically bite through the minutes until it was nearly twenty after. At that moment the field telephone rang over on the kitchen counter. She heard the ring but she sat there looking at the army green telephone until it rang again, and again. She looked through the window and saw Ken come out into the shade on the east side of the garage and glance towards the house, directly at her sitting in the window. He cupped his hands to his mouth and yelled for her to take the call and then, as though giving instructions to a simpleton, he mimed just how she should go about doing it, pretending to pick up the receiver and jam it to his ear. Finally, rousing herself out of her lethargy, she dragged herself over to the counter and picked up the receiver of the field telephone.

Ken's voice crackled over the line. "Why the heck didn't you ring me? It's almost five-thirty."

Ethel did not reply. She just listened to his voice coming in from Battle Station 1 over to Headquarters, a distance of some thirty feet that seemed more like thirty miles.

"For godsake, Ethel, can't you hear me? I asked you why you didn't ring me?"

At that moment, something welled up in her breast that nearly brought sobs. "Because I'm all rung out," she told him, and hung up. When the phone rang again she unscrewed the terminal nuts and yanked off the wires.

If anything had the effect of putting some hustle into her Ken it was the sin she just committed. Less than a minute later she heard the aluminum screen door pull back. Ken's feet clanked down the hall. He careened around the corner and stood there, sniffing at the air like some animal that had just come in from a sawdust storm. "What's the matter? I don't smell anything cooking," he said.

Her Ken was a good three inches shorter than she was. His right eyeball was all smeared around like something that had been put through an Osterizer, because of some shrapnel that had caught up to him during the War. The blue iris was swirled around in the white. When they first met she asked him why he didn't wear a patch over his eye and he told her pointblank, if the world didn't care to look at what it had done to him then the world could go stuff itself in a doughnut hole. Now, to look at him standing in the doorway, working his nose around like some animal trying to pick up a scent, she found his eye detestable. He was standing there all tough and spare like a leather baseball mitt no one had oiled in a long time, with wrinkles only around his eyes. His arms hung slack from his T-shirt, with those obscene tattoos of girls coiled by serpents on his forearms. Despite his grey hair that was getting a little too long at the back, he looked almost youthful, whereas she knew she had gotten flabby and looked much older than her sixty-three years. No wonder he fools around with girls, she told herself. I'm so frumpy. But then she hardened inside, suddenly hating his hard, tight body and snuffing nose.

"If you want anything to eat just damn well fix it yourself," she said, and loped clumsily toward the bedroom, knocking aside a chair with her large hips.

She lay in the semi-dark a long time, willing Ken to come into the bedroom to see what the matter was. Sunshine lay against the curtains. It was smouldering hot and every once in a while a bead of sweat rolled through the hair at her temples, repelling her. Ken gave no sign of coming in to see her. She tossed her body around on the mattress hoping the sound of the bedsprings would put the suggestion in his mind, but he was as deaf to it as a knot in a pine board. She could hear him clanking pots and pans and now she heard the electric whine of the can opener. No doubt he had chalked up her actions to being "in a mood." As he had told her shortly after they were married: "I leave it to women to figure out why they do the dang things they do. If you're in a mood just tell me and it'll save us both a lot of guessing."

By now she could smell garlic and onions frying on the stove, a hideous smell that nonetheless made her mouth drool. Hunger knifed in her stomach; it annoyed and upset her because she figured the least her body could do was to be loyal to her anger.

Finally she shouted at him, in a tone she hoped would cut: "Just what are you cooking out there anyway? It smells horrible."

There was no immediate reply and she figured she might be forced to holler even louder. But then the door shoved back by just a little and Ken stuck his head around it. "My usual, beans and weiners, smothered in onions."

"God, can't you ever come up with anything else?"

"You know, if I had my way I'd live on beans and weiners. They're just fine with me. And anyway, you don't have to eat them if you don't want to. I'm not going to force you."

"No, you never force me to do anything, do you?"

"Now what do you mean by that, Ethel?"

"You guess," she snapped at him.

He pushed back the door all the way. "Listen, if you've got your octane up over something you just come right out and say so. Don't beat around any bushes. But right now I got to look after dinner so it won't burn."

"Sure, go right ahead and look after your stinking dinner." Then as he scooted down the hallway, just about to turn the corner into the kitchen, she yelled, *"Mr. Fornicator!"*

The next few minutes were deadly silent, all except for him scraping around his smelly garlic and onions in the frying pan. She heard him get into the cupboard for dishes, followed by him getting utensils out of the drawers and what was probably milk and ketchup out of the fridge. After that there was nothing but the report of his fork as he stabbed his weiners and scraped up his beans. She was determined not to say another word until he said something back to her; she was certain he had heard what she called him and was mulling it over with his goddamn beans and weiners, food he maintained was good enough for him in the navy and would be good enough for him from now until eternity if she ever got tired of cooking fancy meals.

"I take it you're not fixing to come out and eat," he finally called to her, which just about fried her flesh because he had obviously said it to avoid asking her why she had called him a fornicator. Her stomach was full of noise and betrayal as it churned and squirted juices, but she was not about to go out to the kitchen, no siree.

"No, I'm not fixing to eat, *Mr. For-ni-kay-tore,*" she said with deliberate finality.

"Okay then, I'll just finish up these beans and weiners if you don't mind?"

She was obstinately silent.

"I take it by that silence you don't mind if I finish up on this grub out here?"

"You take it right. I wouldn't sit down across from you if I was starving and didn't have a dime to my name."

"Okay then, I'm gonna eat it all. Don't come in here and expect to find any because it's all gonna be gone. Cleaned up and put away. Kaput."

That's just what he did, too. He ate up all the beans and weiners, washed his pots and pans and dishes and walked out the door, leaving her with the obnoxious after-odour of onions and garlic which she could only get rid of by opening all the doors and windows. When she heard the rumble of the Harley-Davidson she knew he wouldn't be coming back for a while. Just as he did every evening after supper he took his bike out for a run. These so-called runs had started shortly after he got the Harley and for several weeks afterward he had come home feeling very full of himself for an elderly man, smelling vaguely of beer and singing this horrid song she could still remember the first two lines of: *I'm a night rider for you, baby / My hog is big and wild*, expecting her to roll over for him so he could top off his evening with a furious bout of sex. Well, she had put a stop to that quick enough, aying if he was going to be out nearly all night he better not come home thinking all he had to do was make his presence felt in order to win her favours. No siree, there wasn't going to be any of that.

Later that night, just before one o'clock according to the digital wake-me-up alarm, she heard him clonk into the house. As usual, he sat out in the kitchen having a beer while he listened to the country-western station on the radio. When finally he came to bed he stretched out like a sluggish lizard, let go a greasy-sounding belch and settled in to go to sleep, his body still chilled by the long ride through the night. She was damned if she would let him get away with that, not under God's blue heaven.

"So did you have fun screwing your little girlfriend?" she said, wishing her tongue were a razor that could physically cut him to ribbons.

"I had a good ride, if that's what you're talking about," he told her, his voice as even-toned as a news broadcaster's.

"Oh, is that what your friends call it — having a ride? How cute."

Here, Ken managed to grumble. "Listen, Ethel, if you're not gonna be civil I'm gonna go sleep out in my studio."

"With a clear conscience, I suppose?"

"For crying out loud," he said in those liquid tones that irritated her so much she could spit, "what the Sam Hill are you going on about anyway?"

"What am I going on about!" she shrieked, suddenly pulling herself up in bed. "I'm going on about that little girl you got pregnant, that one who's young enough to be your daughter."

"Who precisely are you talking about, Ethel?"

"Shirley. She called herself Shirley. Surely you know who I'm talking about?"

Ken let out a yowling laugh that filled up all the darkness in the bedroom. She reached over and switched on the table lamp, one of his that comprised several heads and a number of twisted arms and legs. A dull light washed over Ken's face, which was distorted with laughter. His smeared eye was going around like a crazed ball bearing.

"Just what do you find so humorous?"

Ken tried to contain his laughter. He tossed his head to the right to observe her with his good left eye. "What I find so funny is the fact that you bought it. A perfect stranger tells you I made her pregnant and you went ahead and figured it was true."

"I saw her, Ken. She was so big she looked like she might burst any minute."

"But that doesn't mean I made her that way."

"Oh, no? So why did she come here? Why did she tell me she was going to get you muscled if you didn't own up?"

"Because she was having some fun with you."

"Fun? You call that fun?"

"She thought it was fun. From what she told me you nearly fell over in a faint."

"I did no such thing."

"According to her, you did. But then I take what she says with a grain of salt, just the way you should."

And that had ended it, at least by his standards. He rolled over on his side, away from her, and in a few minutes was snoring in that gurgling way he had. Next morning, over breakfast, she told him she didn't care for the type of friends he was keeping company with, to which he merely shrugged, saying everybody to his own taste, and headed out the door to his damned carving shed. The wires, she noticed, had been reattached to the field telephone, obviously in an attempt to tell her things were back to normal in his way of thinking.

Ethel had worked at the drugstore from nine until two, when the druggist's eldest daughter, who was taking classes at the local community college, took over at the cash register. She drove home in her blue Maverick and parked it at the curb now that they no longer had a garage as such, noticing that Ken hadn't bothered to turn on the sprinkler. If taking care of the yard were left up to him they'd have one of those brown, burned-out lawns that told everyone you didn't care a tinker's damn about anything. In their neighbourhood every lawn was green and people took pride in the shape of each bush and tree. The desire to make things look nice hadn't been lost. At one time even Ken had possessed it, but not anymore. Now she was lucky if she could get him to mow the lawn once every two weeks.

Ethel turned on the sprinkler and went inside where she immediately took off her white uniform and slipped into her cream-coloured toga. Her toga was loose-fitting and she could go around practically naked underneath, the crocheted pattern allowing the breeze in but not the eyesight. She went into the kitchen to make herself some instant iced tea. She sat down at the table with her drink and the needlework magazine she had picked up at the drugstore and that's when she noticed the black motorcycle parked by the picket fence in the alley.

"Damn, if he hasn't got her there," she told herself. She rose from the table and headed outside to the garage to make certain her suspicions were correct. She could hear Ken jabbering away inside in that hep talk or whatever they called it nowadays. He was chattering on like he never did with her and every once in a while she would hear a female voice. She quietly unlatched the gate and went to look at the Harley parked by the picket fence.

She couldn't tell for sure but she figured it was Shirley's. Anyway, they all looked pretty much the same to her, mean and loathsome.

The bay door was pulled down flush to the concrete but she could see where Ken's motorcycle had tracked sawdust coming out and dirt going back in. She unlatched the gate again and went back to the side door and listened to Ken going on in that language that was a mishmash of English and something else. Now she clearly heard a woman's giggle, followed by Ken saying something to the effect that he couldn't get the proper fix on her belly so she'd have to move it around. Ethel could picture the way he wanted Shirley to move her belly and what she saw in her mind revolted her. She banged the door so hard it rattled against the doorstop.

"It's me, Ken. I want to know what's going on in there!"

"Work. That's what's going on in here."

"Open up the door then. I want to see for myself. Right now!"

"Ethel, would you kindly go back to the house and let well enough alone for once?"

"No! I refuse! I want to know what's going on in there."

"Art. That's what's going on in here."

"Like fun it is!"

She imagined all sorts of ways to get in, one of which had to do with pouring gasoline around the garage and setting it on fire. On the side of the garage facing the house was a window Ken had covered with cardboard so she couldn't see inside. A forsythia bush grew in front of it, in a frothy display of waving green leaves. Ethel dragged her toga past the branches, which kept insinuating their tips through the holes in the crochet. Finally with some effort, she reached the window. The window was made up of a dozen or so small panes. She looked for a rock but saw none at hand so she took off her shoe and smashed the heel against one of the panes. The fury it released in her felt so good she whacked several more panes, the glass splattering every which way as she yanked and smashed with the shoe. Inside she could hear the voices of Ken and Shirley, one telling the other he had better do something and the other proclaiming, "God, Ethel, what has got into you now?" Ethel reached through the broken pane and flailed around with her arms until she had the cardboard ripped down. Ken was throwing a canvas tarp over whatever it was in the middle of the garage while the girl Shirley was pulling up her jeans, barely getting them up in enough time to hide the crack in her backside.

"I knew it! I knew it!" she wailed, and banged out another couple panes. She grabbed the interlocking wooden frames and started to shake the window, snarling at them through clenched teeth. She was so furious she didn't feel the glass shards cut into her flesh, not until Ken said something about her getting blood all over everything. She looked at her lacerated arms. For a second the blood dazzled her. She was unable to make sense of what she had just done and what she should do now. There was blood on her toga she knew would never come out unless she put it into cold water in a hurry, but she just couldn't move herself to act. And at that moment, she decided to become mute.

Already Ken was thrashing his way through the forsythia bush. He put his hands on her shoulders trying to steer her away from the window but she wouldn't let him. She held fiercely to the frame, staring straight at Shirley who was now sitting side-saddle on Ken's Harley over by the bay door. The smile on her face was almost smug.

"Come on," Ken kept saying. "We have to get you to the hospital."

But Ethel wouldn't let go of the window frame, not even when he pried at her fingers. Blood was running in rivulets down her forearms to her elbows where it collected in beads before dripping onto her toga or the ground at her feet.

"Dammit, Ethel, let go! Let go, will you?"

She shook her head, taking a perverse pleasure in the pain she was causing herself. Finally Ken ran back around to the interior. He took his handsaw down from the pegboard and started sawing out the short lengths of frame around her hands. She glared past his shoulder which was humping up and down as he pushed and pulled the saw, straight at Shirley who had unzipped her black leather jacket and was running her hands over her swollen breasts and belly while she made lewd faces at Ethel. Had Ethel not decided to become mute only a minute or so before, she would have yelled at Ken to turn around quick to catch Shirley in the act of doing what she was doing. Just before Ken finished sawing through the last frame Shirley zipped up her jacket, high enough to hide her belly but low enough to expose plenty of cleavage. She came sashaying over to the window and gave Ethel a wink behind Ken's shoulder.

"It doesn't look like you'll need me anymore today so I'm gonna get outa here. See you later at the Pit Stop."

"I don't know if I'll make it tonight."

"Why? Because of her? She don't look that hurt."

Ethel couldn't believe it. Here she was bleeding half to death and Ken and this Shirley were debating whether or not they'd meet tonight. Going mute hardly seemed a good enough way to express how upset she was, so she promptly closed her eyes and simulated a faint, crashing backwards into the forsythia bush with the piece of window frame still clutched in her hands. She went down with a thud that was harder than she had expected and was gouged roughly in the back and side by what felt like a stick. The branches rustled overhead and she could identify the light patterns through her eyelids. Soon she heard Ken come thrashing through the forsythia. She felt his thumb on her eyelid, then she found herself staring into his muddled right eye. She tried to make her own eye look dead, the same way a fish's eye looked dead. Ken let go her eyelid and went thrashing back through the forsythia and soon she heard the screen door bang shut. She heard Shirley's bike thunder down the alley, and opened her eyes. It seemed so peaceful lying there under the swaying branches, with the sky flashing in blue patches. A tiny little bird fluttered into the bush and proceeded to hop from branch to branch, calling to mind a song she had once heard that compared love to a bird that spread its little wings and flew away. She wanted to weep. Darned if she didn't. But she knew if Ken came out and saw tears running down her cheeks her faint would have been for nothing.

After what seemed a long time she began to wonder if Ken was going to leave her to rot under the forsythia bush. It was getting uncomfortable lying there and her arms were beginning to dart with so much pain she found herself gritting her teeth.

She was mulling over whether to call off her faint when she heard the screen door bang again, and closed her eyes. Moments later Ken came crashing back through the forsythia.

"Are you still out cold?"

What was she going to do, answer him that yes she was? He fought his way back through the bush and returned a short while later and now Ethel heard him sawing off branches of the forsythia. That just about pained her as much as her lacerations. She could see in her mind's eye what the forsythia was going to look like, like one of those punk rockers with their hair shorn off in ugly swaths. She wondered if all the attention she was getting right now would be worth the looks of the bush later on. Then she heard the siren. Obviously Ken had gone into the house to phone for an ambulance. She listened to the siren approach, trying to calculate how long it would take and how much more damage Ken could do to the forsythia bush.

The next day, Ethel would find that the bush had been all but cleared out on one side. Ken couldn't have done a better job of mutilating it if he had lobbed in a hand grenade. By then her arms would be wrapped in gauze and tape to the elbows and the tips of her fingers would jut like sausages out of bandages on her hands and she would ask herself: for what? Because Ken would be back out in his damned old carving shed whittling away at whatever it was under the canvas tarp, again with the cardboard tacked up over the window.

All the way to the hospital and back, she had kept her vow to stay mute. She didn't answer any questions. She gripped the piece of window frame to her breast and wouldn't release it until they had put her on the table in the emergency room and even then it had taken several minutes of pleading by one of the nurses to get her to give it up. But throughout it all she hadn't uttered so much as a word or whimper. She remained stony in her silence even when the doctors and nurses probed her lacerations for splinters of glass. It had taken nearly thirty stitches to close the wounds. When the doctor asked her if she had been having an argument with her husband she simply looked past his shoulder, off into space. Let him think whatever he wanted, let him think that Ken was some kind of glass-wielding wife-beater. It didn't matter to her, not anymore.

Later when Ken was allowed to take her home he had been contrite and almost what she might call doting. He opened the car door and helped her scoot inside and drove slowly all the way home so as not to jostle her around too much. At home he made certain she was comfortable in bed; he asked her whether she needed another pillow and whether she wanted a glass of water on the nightstand, questions she responded to with nods or shakes of her head. It had given her a feeling of victory. But the next morning that victory was wrested from her the moment Ken got up from the breakfast table, poured himself a cup of coffee and trudged out to the garage. She sat at the kitchen table and watched him unlock the door to his studio and disappear inside and she knew all the ground she had gained had been lost. But even then, she didn't speak. She remained irrevocably mute and stubborn in her silence.

That morning she did not go to work. The druggist phoned her at home but because she had vowed to stay mute she couldn't explain to him why she wouldn't be showing up at work. Twice he phoned; both times she held the receiver to her ear, listening to him say: "Ethel, Ethel, is that you on the other end of the line? What's happened? Are you all right?" But she couldn't answer him and so she hung up. Then, so she wouldn't get any more phone calls, she yanked out the cord. After all, a telephone would be useless to her now. She wrote a note to that effect and set the phone on it on the kitchen counter, along with instructions for Ken to return it to the phone mart. She went outside to turn on the sprinkler so the grass would remain green and then she sat down in the Lazy Boy armchair and tried with her swollen, aching hands to crochet a new toga to replace the one that had been stained with blood.

Around ten o'clock the doorbell rang and when she opened the door she found a policeman on the stoop. The policeman told her that the druggist had phoned the station and was worried that maybe something had happened at the Rimley's because she hadn't shown up for work and whoever picked up the telephone had refused to answer. "We thought we'd better check it out," the policeman said, glancing down at her forearms in the gauze and tape. He was a young man, the kind you wouldn't mind having as a son. She nodded her head and attempted to close the door, but he held it open.

"Mind if I have a look around?" he said. "Just to make sure?"

She shrugged in a manner that said she didn't care. He strolled into the house and systematically went through each room; he caught sight of the telephone on the kitchen counter, read the note she had written to her husband and asked where her husband was. Ethel took him to the kitchen window and nodded towards the garage. He said thank you, tipped his cap and went out the back door and down the concrete walkway to the side door and knocked. He knocked several times before he finally got Ken to open up. The policeman ducked inside. Later he came out with Ken. Both Ken and the policeman were sharing some joke because they were both laughing as they headed around the house.

Once the police car was out of sight down the street, Ken turned and marched straight into the house. When he saw Ethel standing at the front window he shook his head rapidly back and forth. "I don't know what's got into you, Ethel. You're getting as crazy as some hoot owl."

He went past her into the kitchen. Ethel followed him. He walked straight over to the telephone, quickly read the note, then plugged in the cord. "You might not want to use it ever again, but I might."

She stared at him, trying to waylay him with her silence.

"What the hell are you trying to prove anyway? Whatever it is I don't buy it. I'm not going to be one of those old men who totter around on canes making sure they don't stumble on any cracks in the sidewalk. That seems to be what you want out of me, but that's not what you're gonna get. Do you understand? You're not gonna catch me sitting in any goddamn Lazy Boy waiting for the end. When I go it's gonna be like lightning struck me down. And I'm gonna keep on carving, and if I need models for that I'm gonna go out and get them and you're not gonna stop me. Do you hear? Do you hear me, Ethel?"

Because she had taken a vow of silence she couldn't reply. Even if she had allowed herself to speak she saw how useless it would be trying to explain to him because he was so furious and unreasonable and wanted things only his own way. He wanted to ceaselessly drag his sawdust and wood chips into the house, where she always had to vacuum them up. He wanted the company of his damned old carvings more than he wanted her company. To her, every one of his carvings represented how basically selfish he had become. It wasn't any of this other high-minded malarky. It was just selfishness, and now he figured he should be able to bring his whores home too, on top of it. Well, she was not having any of it, no siree.

Ken whacked a cup off the counter into the sink. The cup splattered in fragments. He stormed out of the house, slamming the door as hard as he could. Ethel yanked out the phone cord and proceeded to pick up the china shards in the sink. She was rinsing the tinier shards down the drain when she heard the Harley-Davidson kick over, and went to the window to see Ken go barrelling off with his grey locks snapping in the breeze. Well, he could just ride that thing straight on to hell as far as she cared, because that was where he and his creative juices belonged, sizzling over some everlasting fire.

Ethel went into the bathroom. There in the tub was her toga, soaking in cold water and bleach. The blood-soaked areas had not become white. They had turned bluish and resembled some disfigured spirit she was trying to exorcise with Purex. She recalled her first glimpse through the broken window the day before, how she had caught Shirley pulling up her jeans while Ken was throwing the tarp over his precious so-called masterpiece. She had stood there watching them, blood flowing down her arms, glass slicing into her flesh. Ethel tried to raise the toga to see if the blood stains would come loose. With all the water in the fabric the toga weighed a ton. It was too heavy for her lacerated arms to lift very far out of the tub, but she saw by lifting out part of it that the stains had set quite firmly. She let the toga slide back down into the water and went to the kitchen, too angry to sit down at the table to drink a cup of coffee. She looked out the window at Ken's studio and the very sight of it was enough to make her visualize blowing it up, with Ken and his whore of a girlfriend inside. What had he thrown the tarp over anyway? She thought she had caught a glimpse down at the bottom where Ken had had to give the tarp an extra little tug to unfold it over what seemed to be a wooden tire. By now her anger was something hard and impelling, like a fist swollen in her throat.

How could he just ride off like that? Didn't she mean anything to him anymore?

She pushed back the screen door and went down the concrete walkway to the garage. Ken had recently installed a padlock and, of course, it was locked. So was the bay door. She went back around to the window where she had smashed out the panes. She reached inside and tore away part of the cardboard only to find Ken had nailed slats across the window. Ethel returned to the house and got the hammer and screwdriver she kept in one of the kitchen drawers. She went back out to the garage and banged at the slats. The jarring impact sent pain rippling through her arms, but her anger let her ignore it. Finally a slat fell off. By now several of her wounds had begun to weep, the gauze soaking up the blood in frayed-looking splotches. She looked coldly at the blood and went on with her work. Half an hour later she had all four slats off the inside of the window. She whacked out several more panes of glass, taking delight in the destruction, then she beat at the interlocking frames until she had made a hole she figured was large enough to get her body through. She returned to the house for a chair and set it under the window and climbed up on it in order to crawl through and that's when she noticed the man next door, staring at her from between tepees of pole beans.

"Nice day we're having," he said, tipping his rumpled felt hat. "I've been meaning to ask you if you and your husband would like some beans and zucchini. We got way more than we can eat ourselves."

Ethel looked at him with a face that could have shriveled the skin off an onion, shook her head rudely and proceeded to climb through the window. Glass crunched underneath her shoes when she stepped down inside the garage. She flicked on the light switch by the door and looked at the mound with the canvas tarp thrown over it. Her insides jerked and heaved and she even trembled. She grabbed the hem of the tarp and pulled it back over the sculpture.

What she found herself staring at was none other than a pregnant woman, naked except for an unzipped jacket, riding one of the meanest-looking motorcycles she had ever seen. The woman's long hair flared behind her, all frilly and tangled in the breeze; her jacket was open and wafting, and her feet were planted far forward on pegs, her knees wide apart, with her monstrous belly spilling forward onto the gas tank. But it was the face that arrested Ethel; it was not Shirley's face, with that pugnose that made her look either cute or ugly. No, the face bore a striking resemblance to Ethel's own face, a face she remembered looking at in the mirror some thirty or forty years ago when she had met Ken in the restaurant where she had been working as a waitress. Indeed, when she looked around the garage she saw some snapshots of her hanging on the wall above the workbench, one of her in a bathing suit, standing beside an outboard boat they had once owned, holding up a fish in either hand. Another was of her standing in front of an old '50 Chevy, with flowers bunched in her arms, smiling a lot like the pregnant woman on the motorcycle.

What in heaven's name could Ken be thinking of, putting her face on such a repulsive piece of sculpted junk, making her look cheap and trashy the way Shirley did, for all the world to look at and wonder what kind of kinky goings-on they might indulge in in the privacy of their bedroom? She was appalled; the spittle of disgust rose in her throat. She wrenched the handsaw from its metal hook on the pegboard and the hook went flying. The first thing she tried to cut off was the right arm of the pregnant biker. When the saw proved no match for her anger she grabbed an axe she saw leaning against the workbench and began to flail at the sculpture with that. The arms and handlebars came off with a flurry of chips. She whacked at the pregnant stomach with the prominent belly button but because she was working against the grain she only managed to take out chunks. She moved around to the other side, hurling the axe repeatedly against the hair that rode on the turbulent breeze; she sliced into the Angel insignia on the back of the jacket and took off a buttock and part of the bike's seat. By this time she was sweating; her fierce breathing came in rasps, the air burning down into her lungs. The face she had looked at so long ago in the mirror she now relieved of the nose and lips, then she pounded nails into it around the eyes, bent them and smashed them until the face was indescribable and ugly. Then she crawled out through the window and returned to the house. She drained the bathtub, wriggled into the wet, slippery-feeling toga with the permanent bluish stains and lay down on the bed she and Ken had owned ever since they first bought and furnished the house. The toga, over the hours she spent staring at the ceiling, gradually relinquished its wetness to the mattress and the mattress began to rain drops on the floor.

According to the digital wake-me-up alarm clock it was nearly one in the morning when Ethel heard Ken's Harley-Davidson rumble down the alley and finally give up the ghost. She heard the bay door of the garage go up and clenched her fists, waiting for what she thought would be the inevitable attack by Ken once he saw what she had done to his damned carving. She visualized him swinging an axe, hacking off her head and arms, making holes in her stomach for her guts to spill through. However, she was determined to just lie there, lie there and accuse him with her silence, as statuesque as one of his sculptures, even smiling.

It was nearly half an hour before Ken shoved back the door and came tromping into the house, straight down the hallway to the bedroom where he switched on the light. He didn't have an axe in his hands, no, he was holding the wooden arms of the pregnant biker, and he was crying, sobbing; tears even brimmed his mutilated eye.

"Damn you, damn you, you ruined my madonna, you killed her, Ethel, you killed her!" he yelled, and turning away from the doorway, he went back down the hall, slamming the aluminum screen door as he left the house.

So it was her? So she was the guilty party, was she? Not in her book. In her book it was him, he was the one who let his damned carving become an obsession that tore apart their marriage. He was the one who had degraded her by putting her face on that obscene angel on the motorcycle. It was him. She had only stood by; she had not changed, he had. She was not the one who wanted to become immortal. He was, he and he alone, an aged man of sixty-seven who would not act his age.

Ethel got up from the bed. In her permanently stained toga, which in its stretched and wet condition dragged along the floor, she headed down the hallway and made the left turn into the kitchen and went straight to the door. Through the screen she saw the flames dancing on the garage window, also the orange splotch on the lawn at the side door. She shoved back the screen and hurried down the steps to find Ken in order to tell him she was going to phone the police. But when she got to the side door she saw that would be useless. Ken was sitting on the sculpted motorcycle, belly to belly with the angel, clasping her with his tattooed arms, hugging her carved body with the fierceness of a lover, his head turned and resting on her shoulder, his scrambled eye peering quite serenely at Ethel as he went up in flames.

Ethel thought of those Hindu women who threw themselves on their husband's funeral pyres; the thought caused her to shudder. She drew back from the flames in the doorway and stood watching at a safe distance, while far-off a siren unwound like a bright ribbon through the night.

MOVING THE PATRONE'S APPLE TREE

Alex Kuusi could not at first make sense of his surroundings. He seemed to be floating off-kilter, as though at the end of a long tether. And yet, at the same time, he seemed to be somewhere downhill from the Patrone's house, staring up through the branches of the apple tree at the Victorian facade. Possibly he was standing on the sidewalk. But if that were the case, where was the Patrone's fence? And what had become of the oblong wooden container he had built beside the driveway to hold the Patrone's garbage cans? From what he could tell it was another drab Vancouver day. His hands were sunk deep in his trouser pockets and his breath was issuing in gossamer plumes from his nostrils. Somehow his children had got themselves up into the apple tree and were crawling around in the branches, screaming at the top of their lungs. Ester and Heddy had on nightgowns and red mittens and little one-year-old Ben was wearing his white crash-helmet. They were having a good time, but Alex was getting anxious for them to come down lest the Patrone see them. Indeed, he was just about to shout for them to do so when, in slow-motion, a bolt of lightning arced down from somewhere in back of his right shoulder and struck, with pinpoint accuracy, the trunk of the tree. The top exploded in a myriad of fireworks and his children, thrown high into the air, now began a tumbling descent towards him on the ground.

"No!" he shouted, jerking up in bed and hurling out his arms to hold back what was happening. "No!" he yelled, and wrenched open his eyes, only to find himself struck by a wedge of light coming from the hallway. The warmth had drained from his face, his cheeks hung slack and his lips were writhing like halves of an earthworm severed by a spade. For a few moments he sat there utterly confused, still gripped by the terror of seeing his children hurled through the air. Gradually, as the dream became less vivid, his fear began to subside. He was able to fasten on particulars of the room. He noticed the blankets thrown back on the other side of the bed and he heard, coming from beyond the wall behind him, the faint but rhythmic creaking of the rocking chair, and now his wife's voice, angelically crooning a lullaby.

Alex glanced at the digital alarm clock on the nightstand and saw by the glowing red numbers it was shortly after three in the morning. He had got into bed around twelve o'clock, after tiling the bathroom floor. He had intended to do the tiling on the weekend, but after working all day for the Patrone he had found himself too agitated to settle down. He had thought by tiling the floor he would be able to wear himself out sufficiently to eventually fall asleep. He knew it wasn't by accident that he had dreamed of the Patrone's apple tree. Three years ago he had moved it from a site down on 3rd Avenue up to its present location on 10th. Then only yesterday he was informed he would be moving it again: from the front yard of the Patrone's house to the far corner of the backyard. The Patrone said he wanted it done as cheaply as possible and that, to the Patrone, meant only one thing: labour, back-breaking labour, and Alex would be supplying that.

Except for the strange off-kilter feeling that wouldn't seem to go away, he had nearly put the dream behind him. But his nerves were beginning to buzz and he knew it would be impossible to go back to sleep, at least for the next half-hour or so. He dragged himself out of bed and, pulling on his robe, went to see what had got Angey up. Earlier, when he had finished tiling the bathroom floor, his back had been aching so much he had put off cleaning up the mess until morning. There were all sorts of broken tiles scattered around in the hallway outside the bathroom door. A cutter and a pail with hardened thin-bed mortar had been left to steer traffic around the shards. Even though he followed the path he had made, he managed to put his foot down on a splinter which pricked him behind the ball of his big toe. Before he could stop himself he had muttered a grumbling curse.

In what they referred to as the living room he heard his wife stop singing. "So what is it now?" she said with a piercing nasal whine. "What are you swearing at now?"

"Nothing I just stepped on a piece of tile."

"Well, why swear about it?"

"Because it was sharp," he said, "and because it's stuck in my foot."

"Well, it serves you right for not cleaning up, doesn't it?"

Alex did not reply. He leaned his butt against the wall and, yanking his foot up until his right leg was in the half-lotus position, he tried to locate the offending shard. It was a sharp little devil, thin as a sliver of glass, and he found himself squinting as he squeezed it between his fingernails and pulled it out. He held it up to the light, amazed at how thin it was. The tip looked as if it had been broken. He tested his foot on the floor to see if it had been left in his flesh. There was a miniscule prick but he knew that could be due to the wound. He rolled his foot around on the ball several times just to make sure, then flicked the splinter into the pail of hardened mortar, headed on through the golden yellow kitchen and turned the corner into the diminutive living room at the back of the house. His wife had resumed the lullaby, only now she was humming rather than singing. He found her sitting in the rocking chair in the semi-dark, his son's head resting on her bosom, her pale hand soothing the nape of his neck. Just as Alex stepped through the door his son twitched several times and uttered a series of whimpers reminiscent of a dog having a dream.

"So what's the matter with him?" Alex said, knowing instantly he should have framed the question so it sounded more sympathetic.

"His ears," Angey said, looking up at him with a long-suffering expression.

"His ears? I thought he just got over a cold in his ears."

"That was a few weeks ago."

"Well, how can he get another one so soon? I thought that's why we were buying him all that penicillin—to avoid this sort of thing."

Angey just turned her head away, staring off into the darkest corner she could find, which happened to be the corner with the faulty fireplace. He had discovered just how faulty it was the first time he tried to use it. He had bought several Duraflame logs, thinking Angey and he might spend a romantic evening sitting in front of the fire. When he set the logs ablaze the room quickly filled with smoke that spread to other parts of the house. The problem turned out to be a concrete plug in the chimney, which he figured a previous owner had installed when the upstairs was turned into a suite. The flue terminated roughly beneath the refrigerator on the third floor. It was one of many such features he had run across over the four years he had owned the house.

"So what did you yell about?" Angey said, now turning her gaze from the fireplace.

Alex brought his mind back from where it had gone. He looked at his wife who was petting little Ben's head. Her deep-set eyes glistened like obsidian. Somehow they had the uncanny ability to drill right into him. "It was nothing, just a dream."

"Obviously not a very pleasant one."

"I don't want to talk about it. I think I'll clean up the mess I made before someone gets hurt."

On his way to the kitchen he sat down at the table and upended his foot again and tried to locate the spot where the splinter had gone in. He could still feel a little tenderness in the ball of his foot. But even though he pressed around the area he could not seem to find the exact spot of entry. There was no blood or obvious little hole. Finally he gave up looking, deciding that if there were a bit of splinter in his foot it would just have to work its own way out. He found the dust pan and began to scoop up broken tiles and deposit them into the box they had come in, trying not

MOVING THE PATRONE'S APPLE TREE

to make any more noise than necessary. Though he owned the house, thanks to the Patrone, it wasn't his to roam around in as he pleased, making all sorts of noise that might bother his tenants. The tenants were a requisite part of the plan, for without them he could little afford to pay off the mortgage each month.

The tiles weren't exactly the colour he would have chosen for the bathroom. They were a dark-brown, non-slip variety and he would have preferred something in pastel, with a bit of gloss to it. But they were in his price range, being leftovers from a job he had done for the Patrone a couple months earlier, in the foyer of an apartment building in the East End. The carpet had been riddled with burnholes, thanks to tenants grinding out cigarettes on it, and the Patrone had decided to replace it with tiles. Alex had made sure on ordering them that he had included enough square feet to do his bathroom floor. He didn't think of it as stealing so much as getting back at the Patrone for all the misery the man had caused him, the least of which was the house in which Alex had invested a substantial part of his life.

Alex had given Sid Yarborough the title of Patrone after reading a novel by some Italian. It suited the man to a tee: he was wealthy, a landowner and vaguely eccentric — one of those people who could afford to cater to his gratuitous whims. Alex was his boy. It was a role he had come to adopt shortly after he got out of the University of British Columbia. He had taken a Master's Degree in Education only to discover it was the wrong profession to be in when the government began to "downsize" it a year later. He had answered a want ad in the newspaper, one for a person who could work flexible hours as a handy man. Alex had talked himself into the services of Yarborough and had been working for him ever since. If, in the beginning, he hadn't known too many tricks of the trade, he certainly did now. Many of those tricks had been learned at Yarborough's expense. But Yarborough deserved it, he figured, after sticking him with the house. He had hoped to get out of the situation after a year or so, but housing prices had dropped so dramatically he couldn't sell without incurring a loss he might never get out from under.

The way he had entered the deal was fairly simple. Yarborough had offered to extend him a loan of twenty thousand dollars, coupled with a phony letter indicating that Alex was his personal project manager and would be earning over forty thousand a year. On the strength of those two items Alex had obtained a mortgage for the house, which Yarborough had more or less handpicked for him. Alex figured there were two major reasons why Yarborough had chosen that particular place: one was the colour, which was the same as Yarborough's house; and the second was the location, which was two blocks away and easy to keep an eye on. Shortly after the deal had gone through the two of them were sitting in Yarborough's living room toasting their joint deception. Suddenly Yarborough turned on the sofa and fondly draped his arm along the back and looked through the window down the street in the direction of Alex's house.

"You know, when the leaves fall off the trees I should be able to see right down into your living room," he said with an ironic laugh. "Yes, sir, it's a nice location, here in the heart of Kitsilano. I would count myself lucky if I were you."

Something about Yarborough's tone had made Alex feel much less fortunate than he had felt only moments earlier, and in the succeeding years Alex had come to understand why. Though their houses were only two short blocks away from each other, those two blocks made all the difference in the world, especially as far as housing prices went. The back of Alex's short lot had a wedge taken out of it by 10th Avenue, which made a sudden jog up to 12th. The northeast corner of his house sat less than ten feet away from the busy thoroughfare, whereas Yarborough's house was, by contrast, located on a relatively quiet residential street. The traffic going past Alex's house was so unremitting that Angey was afraid to let the children outside to play. In an attempt to remedy the situation Alex had erected a fence around their postage-stamp back yard, intending in time to put up a swing set and to build a sandbox. About a month after he put up the fence the city sent him a letter ordering him to tear it down because it obstructed the view of drivers coming out of the alleyway behind his place. Yarborough had watched the fence go up, offering a condescending shake of his head. "Wasted effort," he had commented at that time. "That's all kids will ever get you." Alex had thought that Yarborough was simply being sarcastic. He was aware of the man's deep fear and loathing of children. It came out not only in disparaging remarks, but also in nasty grimaces he gave them whenever he found himself in their proximity. Yarborough was forty-one, seven years older than Alex. He was the sort of guy you'd expect to see advertising electric shavers on television. Manly but with well-crafted features, he had a dimple in his chin which squeezed shut whenever he was in the throes of deep concentration. He lived with a woman twelve years his senior, one who paid him rent each month. Their suite was the epitome of an art-deco lifestyle, all of it designed and upholstered in order to compliment this enormous diptych of a voluptuous-looking iris about to be consumed by the darkness of hideous desire.

It might have been coincidence that Alex's house was the same light grey-green colour as the Victorian one on the hill. Alex had no way of knowing how much of a factor this had been in Yarborough's decision to put down money on the place. But lately Yarborough had been talking about repainting his house. When he told Alex to price the job he dropped the hint that Alex figure out how many square feet his house was and that they paint both their houses at the same time. "But Sid, my house doesn't need a paint job."

"What do you mean? Your paint job is worse than mine. Just look at the way the porch is peeling, and up top where the dormer is. It needs a paint job, Alex. It needs one in the worst way."

"Yes, but my bank account doesn't need it. I'm still reeling from that laundry room I put in."

"But that had to be done. Your house was sagging at the back." This was true, the house had been sagging at the back, because of some rot where the walls sat on pedestal blocks. Alex had intended only to jack up the house and put in a proper foundation at the rear. But Yarborough had told him he might as well dig out the old store room and put in a nice laundry which would increase the value of the house. So Alex went ahead and did it. It didn't cost all that much more. Also, his wife found it handy having laundry facilities downstairs. But it had resulted in some lean months he was only now beginning to recover from. So the suggestion that he paint his house was not very welcome and he said so, point-blank. Yarborough only shook his head. "I appreciate your position, but I do have to look after my investment. If you let your paint job deteriorate, the value of your house is going to plummet and to tell you the truth, I don't think I can afford that."

At this point, the conversation was cut short by a telephone call. "Just a minute, Vic." He wrapped the receiver in his palm and turned to Alex. "We'll talk about this later. Meanwhile, why don't you find out what's wrong with Bev's sink."

Bev was the tenant on the top floor of Yarborough's house. Though Yarborough was wealthy enough to afford a house several times over, a parsimonious streak in his character made him put up with tenants on three of the four floors, even though he admitted hating to deal with them in any way. Again, that's where Alex, the ultimate handy man, came in. He took care of those who were obstinate or hard to deal with. On one occasion, when a particularly foul-mouthed tenant had fallen behind on the rent of a basement suite, Yarborough had sent Alex in to make what he called a few repairs. What Alex had been told to do was remove the toilet and put it in the side yard. When that failed to get the proper results Alex was sent back to remove the gas range and to do some electrical repairs which left the suite without any electricity. It was amazing how a few repairs of that nature could solve certain problems. Alex remembered the ghoulish wink Yarborough had given him on successful completion of the job. "Yes, I think you're going to work out all right," he told Alex over a glass of whiskey. "You're not one of those bloody idealists with a cream-filled centre. You've got the right stuff."

Alex glanced at Angey as she went by in the hallway. Ben's little noggin bounced on her shoulder as she disappeared with him into the children's room at the front of the house. At one time when the house had been a single family dwelling, that room had been the parlour. Now it was crammed to capacity with beds and dresser drawers and paraphernalia peculiar to small children. When the kid-stuff stayed put in the kids' room the situation was tolerable. But more often than not that wasn't the case. The kids were like waist-high tornadoes that left toys, blankets, books and cookie crumbs strewn in their wake. Angey was always trying to bring order to the prevailing chaos, and more than once, on coming home from work, he had found her sunk in a corner on the floor, weeping in despair over the tumult around her.

Alex knocked the hardened mortar out of the plastic pail. It fell into the box with the tile scraps, producing a sound not unlike that of breaking dishes. When his wife returned from the kids' room she stood leaning in the bathroom doorway surveying the tile job. "So when do you put the toilet back?" she said, giving the drainhole with the cloth wadded into it a significant look, one which bordered on hostile. Alex had stuck the toilet in the bathtub. With Angey's pink showercap on top of the water closet, the toilet resembled an elderly woman of advanced weight trying to conceal herself behind the shower curtain.

"I'll have it in by morning."

"So I guess I just have to hold it until then. Is that right?"

"I don't see any alternative, not unless you want to get inventive."

"I'll just hold it," she said, and turned to go into the bedroom, her body slouched in that long-suffering posture which never failed to rouse his guilt. He finished cleaning up the mess and took the box of debris out to the rear landing, only to discover the landing cluttered with empty pop bottles, on top of which Angey had balanced the wire shopping cart she took nearly everywhere she went. Once when he came home he found the suite unoccupied. After half an hour he went looking for his brood. Eventually he found them trooping down the sidewalk on Broadway, looking for all the world like a band of derelicts, one that was being led by a bag lady. The sight of them had made such a dismal impression he had taken them out for dinner at the local MacDonalds, simply to assuage his feeling of blame over how poor they were.

Alex took the box of broken tiles down to the laundry room, realizing when he got to the door that he had forgotten the key.

He left the box beside the door and hurried upstairs to the kitchen and removed the key from its hook on the inside of the cupboard door. Instead of going back down empty-handed he took two boxes of empty pop bottles and stowed them with several others in the laundry room, which was beginning to overflow with such items. At one time he had thought of using the other half of the room as a workshop in order to do some small engine repairs in his spare time. They could always use the extra money. But that was why he had gone back to school, to get out of that sort of rut. To start doing small engine repairs again was like admitting failure, so he had given up on the idea.

His Tradesman van was parked in the backyard approximately where he had intended to put the swing-set. He decided since he was up doing things he might as well haul some of the junk out of the laundry room and fill up the back of the van. The next day he would cart the stuff over to the East End and chuck it in a dumpster behind one of the Patrone's apartment buildings. A light drizzle was coming down and he could feel the shoulders of his robe getting wet as he hauled stuff to the van. It was typical weather for May. He would be out working in it all day at the Patrone's and he figured he might as well prepare himself for it.

The first time he had moved the apple tree was three years before during the month of November. He had arrived at the Patrone's house thinking he would go through the formality of discussing the day's activities and then head off to the East End to finish painting a suite which was going to be occupied on the 15th. Instead, Yarborough had informed him there was a slight change in plans.

"What sort of change?" Alex had said, hoping it wouldn't be one of those repair jobs that necessitated removing a tenant's toilet or range.

"A little transplanting job. You know my place down on 3rd. Well, there are a couple fruit trees out back. An apple and a pear. What I'd like you to do is move them up here."

"That apple tree's awfully big, Sid."

Yarborough shrugged off the size. "I suspect you can trim it back a little. What I want you to do is put it where the maple is.

You know, that one that's dying in the front yard. We can deal with the pear later on."

"Listen Sid, do you know what the roots on that apple tree are going to be like? They're going to be extensive, really extensive. We'll have to rent a high-it just to get the tree over here."

"What's a high-it?"

"A flat-bed with a telescopic crane."

Yarborough shook his head. "No, I don't want any of that. This has to be done at minimal cost. Stephanie's kid can help you if you need some assistance."

Stephanie was his co-vivant. She was a dedicated aerobics nut who found it fashionable to display Jane Fonda's *Workout Book* on the coffee table. Yarborough never referred to her son as Lewis or Lew. It was either Stephanie's kid or Lewd.

"Well, I had better dig up the maple first," Alex told him. "It'll take a while to get it out."

"Can't you just saw it off at the ground and dig another hole for the apple tree?"

"Where?"

"Right beside it."

"Look, do you figure the roots on that maple are going to be like a carrot's?" The look on Yarborough's face, which was suddenly so blank, told him that's exactly what Yarborough had thought.

"There can't be that many roots," Yarborough said, typically shrugging off any snags. "I mean after all, it's dying. You know that yourself."

"Yes, but look at the size. That maple stands about sixteen feet. The trunk's at least ten inches across. I would bet the roots fan out twelve feet or more."

"You won't know that until you start digging."

"Well, that's what I'm proposing—that we dig up the maple before we yank out the apple."

"I have a better idea. Let's put Stephanie's kid to work. He can dig out the maple while you get started on the apple. Then you can get him to help you with the move. That sounds like a better approach to me."

"Doesn't Lewis have to go to school?"

"Lewd can miss school today. Besides, this will be a better education for him. Isn't that right, Lewd?" Sid shouted in the direction of Lewis' room.

The reply was slow and languid. "What's that, Sid?"

"I said you wouldn't mind missing school today, would you?"

"What for?"

"So you can earn a little extra money."

"I don't need any extra money."

"Are you trying to thwart me, Lewd? You know what I'll do if you thwart me. I'll dream up some way to persecute you — like scrubbing out toilets twice a day."

"I'd be glad to miss school, Sid."

"I thought you'd see it my way."

Mainly what Alex disliked about Lewis was having to babysit him. One had to constantly prod the kid to keep him on task. He was extremely tall, with light blond hair and a cherubic face. He moved so slowly it seemed as if he contemplated each move before making it. Alex figured the kid's lethargy was partly defensive, a way of getting out of work. It was also a way of annoying Yarborough, whom the kid detested. Alex failed to understand how Sid figured he would be saving time and money putting Lewis to work digging out the maple. However, Alex knew by the sadistic look on Sid's face that he was determined to have his way. Alex gave Lewis a shovel and axe and told him exactly what to do. He even went so far as to draw it out on a piece of paper. But later in the afternoon when he came back to secure the kid's help he found Lewis sitting on an upturned bucket poking at the earth the way his own kids would sometimes poke at their meals. In the time it had taken Alex to trim and up-root the apple tree Lewis had managed to sink what were a half-dozen gopher holes, with little mounds of dirt outside each entrance.

Alex shook his head. Lewis smiled up at him from the bucket, his languid expression masking emotion that was undoubtedly more hostile. "Lewis, my boy, I don't think you'd be able to dig your way through a bowl of ice cream even if I gave you a power shovel."

"You want to try me?"

"No, I've got better plans for you. Come on."

They drove over to 3rd. Alex had removed part of the fence along the alley so he could pull the van into the back yard. The apple tree was held upright by two-by-fours he had shoved under the lowest branches. The tall central trunk had been lopped off with a chainsaw, the major limbs cut back until they were about six feet long. Taken altogether, it resembled a stump out of which several thick boa constrictors had launched their contorted bodies towards the sky, only to find themselves riddled by numerous stubby arrows. Even after all the cutting and slashing the tree probably weighed about two-hundred and fifty pounds. There was a large snarl of roots, many of which Alex had to shorten because they had gone under a concrete slab. When Lewis saw the tree he turned around and started to walk home.

"Lewis, you stop dead in your tracks!" Alex shouted at him.

"Or what?"

"Or I'm going to tell your mother to get you neutered. That way you'll really be worthless."

"Go on, Alex. I'm not going to lift that tree. Not for anybody."

"Come on, it isn't that heavy."

"The heck it isn't," Lewis said, and headed for home. It took Alex over two hours of work on the Come-Along to finally get the tree up on the van. By then the roof was all dented in from walking around on it. Sap was oozing from the severed trunk and splattering on the rear windows of the Tradesman. By the time he got the tree lashed down with ropes he figured the sap had drained right down to the lopped-off tips of the roots. He knotted some of Heddy's old baby clothes to the limbs and proceeded to haul the tree back to Yarborough's place. A few blocks later he was pulled over by a cop who wanted to know how far he was taking the tree. "I know it must look pretty ridiculous," Alex told him. "But the guy I work for is like that."

"Just tell me how far you're going."

"Tenth. A couple houses up from the corner."

"So how did you get that tree up there?" the officer said, raising an eyebrow in its direction.

"Force. Brute force."

Rather than giving him a ticket the officer escorted him to Yarborough's house. When Alex parked the van in the driveway and went to get Lewis to help him with the tree he couldn't find the kid anywhere around. There was some evidence that Lewis had dug a few more gopher holes at the foot of the maple; however, in doing so he had filled in some of the holes he had already dug. Alex tore at his hair. It was almost six o'clock and he envisioned himself working until eleven or twelve that night. He was damned if he was going to haul the tree off the van and over the fence all by himself. The Cadillac was parked in front of his van so he went to get Sid. He found Sid in the office having a drink with Vic Loney, an old fraternity brother with whom Sid had some dealings at the local stock exchange. Vic was a wiry little guy who still played hockey for the fun of it. A bottle of scotch was sitting on the table between them. Alex very casually twisted off the cap and took a big swig and put the bottle down with a thud.

"Your apple tree is here," he said, "thanks to no one but me. Now I need your help getting it off my van."

Vic gave a caustic laugh. "I think he's talking to you, Sid."

"Yes, he seems to be looking in my direction, doesn't he?"

"I think so, Sid. He doesn't look very happy either."

"Why are you so unhappy, Alex?"

"Because I just busted my guts getting that tree over here."

"I told you to get Lewd to help you."

"Lewd took off the moment he saw the tree, which was probably the smartest thing he's ever done. Now I need a hand getting it off the van and inside the fence."

Vic Loney cleared his throat. "I think he means you, Sid."

"Tell you what," Sid told him "Why don't you have another drink while we talk about this?"

"That's fine by me," Alex said, "but meanwhile the life's draining out of your tree."

"What do you mean it's draining out?"

"I think if I showed you you'd probably understand."

So the three of them, Sid, Vic and Alex, trooped down to the van. The tree was still spewing sap. It was cascading off the back of the van and rolling down the driveway toward the sidewalk. "Gee, look at it gush," Vic said. "It's shooting out just like a geyser."

"So what is it?" Sid said.

"Sap," Alex informed him.

"Sap?"

"That's right, sap. If this tree were a person you'd know it better as blood and you'd probably faint dead away."

Out of fairness to Yarborough, he wasn't the sort of guy who balked when he was faced with the inevitability of getting his hands dirty. Together the three of them managed to haul the tree off the van and stand it upright against the fence so the sap wouldn't run out. It took Alex six hours, and nearly a whole bottle of Sid's scotch, to remove the maple and replace it with the apple tree. Alex gave the apple a ten percent chance of living and even then he felt he was being too generous. But the next spring the tree miraculously defied the odds by putting out blossoms and even bearing a handful of apples. The next summer it was even more prolific, and by the third year it was producing so many apples they were left to rot in a cardboard box in the garage. In the end, it was the tree's prolific nature that earned it the disapproval of Sid and Stephanie. One day in the fall of the previous year Stephanie had stepped on an apple and had got the squishy remains on the sole of her shoe and at that point she had started thinking in terms of replacing it.

"You mean you want me to move that tree simply because Stephanie got a little brown pulp on her shoe?" Alex had cringed, not pleased at the thought of uprooting it again.

"It's not just that."

"Then what is it?"

Sid looked a little sheepish. "It's just not the right tree, that's all."

"What do you mean it isn't the right tree?"

"I mean it's the wrong one for that spot."

"Why?"

"Because it doesn't go there. It doesn't . . . connect."

"Is that what you think, or is that what Stephanie thinks?"

"It's what we both think. We want something that's more . . . well, more aesthetic."

"You mean a tree that doesn't leave rotten apples on the ground?"

"Now you've got the idea."

"Maybe you ought to try one of those new plastic trees," Alex suggested.

Sid grimaced. "Somehow I don't think you're viewing this with the proper gravity, Alex."

"No, that's just what I am viewing it with. Gravity, the kind that presses down."

"Let's not be sarcastic. We all know how you like tackling these sort of things. And, of course, you have that wonderful green thumb we all admire so much."

Just then, the telephone had rung. Yarborough answered it, and put the caller on hold. "Tell you what, why don't you go take a look at the spot where we want it — the northeast corner. I think there's some rhubarb you'll have to dig up."

By the time Alex finished bolting down the toilet and reconnecting the supply line it was nearly six o'clock. Even though he felt like going back to bed he knew he had better not do so; otherwise he would sleep until midday. He told himself he would go to bed early that night to catch up on his sleep, then he went to the living room and put "Finlandia" on the stereo and waited for the triumphant sounds to invoke the resilience and determination he was going to need to get through another day working for the Patrone. He leaned his head against the back of the sofa, stared at the ceiling and before he knew it he had fallen asleep. The next thing he became aware of was Heddy jumping into his lap. She landed with both knees planted firmly in his groin, producing a pain the magnitude of which threatened to blot out the entire universe. He sat there gasping, holding himself, his face blanched. Gradually the pain subsided, to be replaced by a nauseous grinding in his bowels. The stereo's playing arm had reached the centre of the LP and a monotonous skipping sound filled the room. Heddy, by this time, was standing in the middle of the floor, the fingers of both hands filling her mouth, looking as though she expected the ceiling to fall on her.

"I thought I told you never to jump on me like that," he told her.

"I didn't mean to, Daddy. Really I didn't."

"Then why did you do it?"

Heddy shrugged. "I don't know. I just did."

Alex heard the toilet flush. A little while later Angey appeared in the doorway clutching her nightgown at her neck. "I see you found him," she told Heddy, who turned to glance at her with quivering lips.

"Yeah, and she came down right on ground zero."

Usually Alex found it necessary to seclude himself for the first half-hour of his waking existence. It took him that long to adjust to the trauma of having to face another day. He rose now from the sofa, turned off the stereo and, giving Heddy a pat on the head, made his way to the bathroom. For a while he stood looking at himself in the mirror, thinking perhaps it was the pain that made his swarthy features look as if he had just swallowed something very distasteful. His mouth was stitched shut in a thin line and the heavy stubble made him look quarrelsome. "Smile, it'll make you feel better," he told himself, opening the medicine cabinet and reaching for his razor. He remembered his mother telling him the same thing before she sent him off to school in the morning. Even then he had found it hard to muster the sort of gumption necessary to hurl himself into the confusion outside the door.

By the time he got out of the bathroom and put on his work clothes, Angey had whipped together some griddle cakes and was waiting on Heddy and Ester at the breakfast table. Ester was dressed in a white blouse and a kilt with a large golden bobby pin that kept the flap down. Of his three children she was the one who favoured him the most, both in looks and temperament. There was that knob of chin and that brooding little cloud on her forehead which marked her as a sensitive child. Alex was glad she had been born a girl because any boy with those features had to be twice as tough to survive the taunts and persecution of his chums. Perhaps because of that he had always felt especially tender towards her.

"So how's the parlez-vous coming, Es?"

She shrugged. "All right, I guess."

"Only all right?"

"We have a test today," she said. "I don't want to talk. I have to get in the right mood."

Alex arched his eyebrows over at Angey. They traded a look, one that said: my, but we're serious this morning. Ester was enrolled in the French Immersion Programme. Because the school was a considerable distance Alex had to drive her each morning. Along the way they picked up another child whose mother returned the favor each and every afternoon. The woman drove a brand new Volvo. One Saturday she invited Ester over to play with her daughter Priscilla. Later in the day Ester had come home to announce to them over dinner, "We're poor, aren't we?"

A look passed around the table, from pair of eyes to pair of eyes. The only one who didn't participate in the exchange was little one-year-old Ben who sat in his highchair squeezing squash through his fingers.

"What makes you think we're poor?" Angey said, stabbing some tuna casserole.

"Well, it's simple."

"How is it simple?" Alex said, feeling himself become irritated although he tried not to.

"Well, the Wascoes have a house all to themselves, upstairs and downstairs, and Priscilla and Gregory have rooms all their own."

Angey gave her a concerned look. "Is this something Priscilla told you, darling?"

"No," she said, poking at her green beans.

"Then who told you?" Alex demanded. "Who told you we were poor?"

"Nobody. I just figured it out for myself."

"Well, you just figure something else out too," Alex told her, perhaps a little too adamantly. "We're better off than most people because we own the house we live in, and most people just rent."

Alex felt embarrassed thinking back on his retort. He finished eating his griddle cakes and went down to warm up the van. Pulling back the door and climbing into the cab he felt a painful prick in the ball of his right foot. He turned over the engine and let it idle while he went around with the squeegie wiping rain off the outside of the windows. He noticed the junk in the back of the van and wondered now why he had packed it because he wasn't going to have enough time to take it across town to a dumpster. Presently Ester came down the back stairs carrying a satchel which bumped against her thigh. He opened the passenger door for her and closed it once she was seated. He went around to the driver's side and hopped in. Ester was staring out the side window which was spotted with rain again and something about her mood, which was so somber, so dark, made him want to chastise her.

"Listen, we might be poor, but we're Kuusis. Kuusis."

She turned to regard him with a bland expression. "What did you say?"

"Nothing," he replied, yanking at the gearshift. "It was nothing." He felt stupid for saying it. He didn't know why he had found it necessary. It was almost as if his mouth had opened of its own accord, the same way those bug-eyed fish were always opening and closing theirs. Alex backed the van out into the street and swung it around in the direction of 16th. Once he had dropped Ester and Priscilla off at school he headed the van back around toward Yarborough's. It was only a ten-minute drive at the very most, but he found each morning he was making it last a little longer in order to postpone the inevitable moment when he would have to face the Patrone. Half an hour later he pulled the van up into the driveway behind his employer's Cadillac. He killed the engine and sat numbly looking out the windshield trying to gather enough energy to shove back the door. His gaze fell upon the back bumper of the Caddy. About a year ago he had ground off the rust and had sprayed it with grey paint and already there were telltale signs of rust leaching through.

"I don't see why you don't just trade your Caddy in for one of those sleek-looking Audis?" he had told Sid at the time. "After all, a Caddy is so gauche, don't you think?"

"I like my Cadillac. It has lots of room."

"But Sid, think how much better an Audi would go with your tennis outfit."

Sid had looked at him with an expression that was almost rabid. "Are you making fun of me, Alex?"

"No, no, of course not," Alex had told him, pulling the trigger of the grinder and producing a loud whir. "I just thought it'd be nice doing this to a bumper that was less formidable."

Alex shoved back the door and stepped down from the van, reaching back inside for the clipboard on the cowling. He unlocked the garage where the tools were kept, then went into the house. He felt his guts tightening as he climbed the stairs to Yarborough's office on the second floor. He reminded himself to smile as he pushed back the door. Sid wasn't in his usual place at the desk so Alex let his smile fade, ultimately to be replaced by a scowl. He sat in the chair off to one side of the desk and tried to focus on the sheet of figures attached to the clipboard. When after ten minutes Yarborough hadn't shown any sign of himself Alex rang him up on the telephone.

"Sid Yarborough speaking."

"Alex here. I hope I didn't get you out of bed?"

"Where are you?"

"Where do you think? Down in your office."

"I'm just about to sit down to breakfast. Why don't you come up here this morning."

"Sure thing. I'll be right there."

Alex dropped the receiver in the cradle. He released a large sigh to disperse the anxiety he was feeling and then he headed upstairs to the third floor. He was certain now the tip of the tile shard had broken off in his foot because each starboard step produced a small pain. After his morning visit with Yarborough he was going to take off his boot and see if he could find the sliver. Alex always felt mildly uncomfortable having to meet Sid in the executive suite. He and another fellow had spent five months renovating it according to Yarborough's whims, which were really the whims of Stephanie. The wall between the living room and bedroom had been moved nearly a half-dozen times before it was finally nailed into place. Stephanie had re-upholstered the furni ture in black kid leather and creamy pink fabrics to go with the diptych of the decadent-looking iris that commanded one wall.

Alex knocked lightly on the door and went in. He found Sid in the kitchen making himself a cappuccino at the chrome-plated machine. Sid smiled over his shoulder. "How about joining me?"

"Sure, if it's on your time."

"It's on my time," Sid said, and gave a sarcastic huff. "Come to think of it, when isn't it on my time?"

"Do I hear a note of complaint in your voice, Sid?"

The reply effectively silenced Yarborough. He finished making one cappucino and began the other. "Just wait until you see the cat I'm now the proud owner of," he said.

"I thought you hated cats."

"I do. Stephanie thought we had to have one though."

"You lucky guy," Alex told him.

"You wouldn't think so if you knew what was involved."

"Don't tell me—you have to build it a separate little condo."

"Just about," Yarborough said.

"Well, don't hold me in suspense. What needs to be done?"

"We're going to need a cat window," he said.

"A cat window. You mean, so little pussy can let itself in or out?"

"That's the gist of it."

"I suppose I'll be the contractor for this mega-project?"

"You got it," Sid winked at him.

"Well, do you want me to make this cat window before or after I move the apple tree?"

"After."

Sid finished making the second cappuccino. They repaired to the dining room where they sat at Sid's new acquisition: a glass table with a gold frame. Sid bit into his toast. He pointed to the greyish furball on the pink divan. "That's Sherman."

"Sherman. I like the name. Is he real?"

"Certainly. You should see how he moves."

Sid picked up a matchbook and tossed it at the cat. Sherman jerked to his feet and scampered off across the divan, its gait reminiscent of a swaybacked caterpillar. At the far end of the divan he turned around and stared at them with eyes that were faintly crossed. It was one of those creatures which stirred in you the desire either to cuddle it or to do it irreparable harm. Alex had to admit it went well with the furniture. Had it not been pointed out to him he might have mistaken it for a mohair cushion.

"So how much did Sherman set you back?" Alex said.

"Nothing, and neither will the cat window. It's all coming out of Stephanie's pocket."

"Well, about the apple tree. Have you decided what you're going to replace it with?"

"I think we've decided on a ginkgo."

"A ginkgo," Alex said. "Are you sure you don't want a coconut palm or something like that?"

"Listen, I know what you think of all this. You don't have to press your point."

"Well, I better get started," Alex said, pushing himself to his feet. "Thanks for the cappuccino."

"Hold on, there's been a slight change."

"A slight change?"

"Yes, as far as where we want the apple tree."

"Don't tell me—you want it up here in your living room, in a nice large pot with dancing girls all around it."

"Come on, Alex. Cut that out. It doesn't become you."

"So where do you want the apple?"

"Stephanie and I were discussing it last night. We think the other corner would be better. I drove a stake in the lawn so you'd know exactly where."

"You're sure this is the final resting place?"

"It had better be, otherwise I told Stephanie she'd find her cat buried in the same spot."

"I suppose I would have to perform that deed?"

"Don't worry. I'd give you a bonus."

Alex grinned. "That's really grand of you. Maybe I better hope she changes her mind."

Sid's backyard looked out upon the backside of some pink and taupe apartment buildings, one of which was a co-op. The co-op had numerous exposed balconies with aluminum guard rails around them. Each balcony contained a variety of tacky possessions, one a blue mattress which had been leaning against the rail for at least three months. The view was the major reason Sid wanted to plant trees along the fence line. In case he ever had friends over to play volleyball he didn't want a horde of sprout-eating co-op types scrutinizing his game.

"So what are the chances of you ever doing that?" Alex had said. "I mean, having a volleyball tournament in your backyard?"

"How should I know? I'm speaking hypothetically," Sid had told him. "The important thing is to block out some of that pastel jungle over there."

"I thought you liked those sort of colours?"

"In moderation. This is a whole bloody cliff."

"Maybe you should plant some langara poplars. They'd block out those buildings."

"Yes, but they'd also block out my view of the mountains."

"Well, that's pretty well decimated anyway."

"Not from my top floor suite," he had said. "That's why I can get so much rent for it."

A light, feathery drizzle was coming down. Alex sank the spade into the lawn about four feet away from the stake marking the new site of the apple tree. First he would remove the grass in a wide circle and stack it in a neat pile beside the garage. When that was done he would dig a hole about three feet deep. He attacked the job slowly, trying to develop a rhythm that would make the work easier. But every time he used his foot to shove the spade into the earth a sharp pain went up his leg. He removed his boot and tried to find the splinter. A bump had risen around the point of entry. Even though he probed it with his pocketknife he couldn't find the bit of shard. He put his boot back on and started digging again, humming the part of "Finlandia" where the choir usually came in. The earth was dark and loamy at the top and tended toward golden brown at the three foot mark. He was approaching completion of the hole when Yarborough came trundling around the corner of the house.

"I thought you'd be out front," he called, sailing across the lawn in his yachting whites.

"I thought I'd do things the right way this time, by starting with the hole I'm going to put the tree in."

"You know, I was thinking. How are you going to get the apple back here?"

"Do you really want to know?"

"I wouldn't be asking you if I didn't."

Alex leaned on the shovel and glanced toward the chimney on the gabled roof. "I thought I'd erect some scaffolding on top your house. I'll winch the tree up and swing it around to over here."

"Come on, I'm being serious."

"Okay, I'm going to put it in the wheelbarrow and I'm going to wheel it back here."

"That sounds just about as ridiculous."

"I know. So why don't you hire five guys and we'll carry it on crosspoles."

"Five guys! Why five?"

"Because it's going to take at least that many to move it."

"How about one more guy, and Lewd and myself?"

Alex felt himself becoming exasperated. He tried to recall "Finlandia" but he felt it wafting off away from him. "Look, I know you like doing things the hard way, but I don't think four of us will be able to move that tree."

"Why? You and Vic and I moved it the last time."

"Yes, but it's grown, Sid. It's grown one hell of a lot."

"Well, I hate to pull rank on you," Sid said. "But I'm not going to hire five guys, not to move a tree I got for practically nothing."

Alex shrugged. "Okay, suit yourself. But you better be prepared to work."

It took until one o'clock for Alex to uproot the apple tree. By then Sid had run off in his Cadillac in order to attend a business lunch and Alex was left in charge of answering the telephone out in the garage. Alex turned on the radio and sat down to relax while he ate his bag lunch. When by two o'clock Sid had yet to appear Alex went back to the front yard to size up just how he was going to conduct the move. It was going to be awkward. The tree had grown to about twelve feet. It was a lot bushier than it had been three years ago and the root structure comprised a great wad of tendrils, with two very large ones sticking out like horns on either side. Getting the tree out of the hole was the first big problem. Getting it onto something which he could roll was the second, and the third had to do with the step-down to the driveway. The step-down occurred at the gate in the fence, which would make it difficult to maneuver the tree. But once those problems were out of the way it would be reasonably smooth sailing to the back yard.

Alex figured the only way he'd be able to get the tree out of the hole would be if he made a tripod with some two-by-fours. He'd attach the Come-Along to a pulley and winch the tree up a little at a time. Then he'd shove the wheelbarrow under the roots and ease the tree down into the bucket. It took him a half-hour to build the tripod. He wired layers of cardboard to the trunk, secured a cable and started to winch the tree slowly up out of the hole, cutting loose some roots still lodged in the earth. Every six inches or so he threw boards under the roots in case the cable gave and the tree came back down. When at last he got the tree out of the hole he found he had under-estimated how tall he should have built the tripod. He couldn't achieve enough height to get the wheelbarrow under the roots. That's when he heard the Cadillac turn into the driveway. He looked up in time to see the car shoot past the gate. Moments later a door slammed and Sid came strolling into the front yard, a briefcase in his hand. He took one glance at the tripod and began to beam.

"Ingenious. Truly ingenious. How long did it take you to come up with this device?"

"All of a second."

Sid came closer. He looked the tripod over, and shook his head in wonder. "Love it, love it. It doesn't look like we'll need that extra guy after all."

"Listen, Sid, this is only the first step. We still have to transport it to the back yard."

"That shouldn't be any problem."

"What do you mean? I've already got a problem."

"What problem is that?"

"I can't get the wheelbarrow under the tree."

"Well, winch the tree up a little higher."

"Can't. The limbs are caught on the tripod."

"Well, what you need is something lower to move it on, maybe a dolly."

"Great idea. I'll run out and rent one."

"Now let's not be too hasty," Yarborough said. Suddenly his face lit up. "I've got an idea."

"What's that?"

"A wagon."

"You don't have a wagon, Sid. At least I haven't seen you playing with it lately."

"No, but you have one. I've seen you pulling your kids around in it."

"You expect me to use my kids' wagon for this?"

"Why not?"

"Because if it gets broken I'm going to have a hard time explaining it to my children."

"We won't break it, not if we're careful."

"Sid, this tree must weigh a ton. It'll smash my kids' wagon to smithereens."

"If it does I'll buy you a new one. Now go get it. I'll roust out Lewd and we'll get started."

Alex decided to walk the two blocks to his house, even though the splinter in his foot sent sharp pains darting up his leg into his groin. The wagon was in the laundry room and he had to go upstaris to the kitchen to get the key. "You're home awfully early," his wife said. "Did something go wrong?"

"Not yet."

He pulled back the cupboard door and took the key off the hook. Ben and Heddy were sitting at the kitchen table, each poised with a marking pen. Ben had on the white crash helmet he practically lived in twenty-four hours a day. Angey had been reading to them when Alex barged in. Now she took a drink from her coffee cup. "I didn't hear the van pull in?"

"That's because I walked."

"Why did you walk?"

"I thought I needed some exercise."

Heddy turned up her nose. "Boy, are you dirty, daddy. How did you get so dirty?"

"Playing around in a hole."

"Why were you playing around in a hole?"

"For the fun of it."

Alex went down to the laundry room. He hauled the wagon outside and was relocking the door when he heard the window slide open above his head. He looked to see his wife gazing down at him. "What are you going to do with the wagon?"

"Pull Sid around the block," he said. "Here, catch the key."

He tossed the key up to her. She caught it in one hand. "You'll be careful with it, I hope."

"You bet." Heddy and Ben had their noses pressed against the window. The smile on Ben's face made him look like some cockamamy little angel. "See you later."

"What's wrong with your foot?"

"Nothing. I just thought a limp would make me look distinguished."

He pulled the red Flyer up to Yarborough's house. Sid and Lewis were waiting for him in the front yard. Lewis was even taller than three years ago. In college he was studying to be some kind of engineer. Sid still had on his yachting whites. He had donned a pair of leather gloves, those that Alex had left on the wheelbarrow.

"Don't you think you better get some old clothes on?" Alex told him, thinking he would snatch back the gloves when Yarborough went to change.

"What for? I'm not going to do the dirty work. You and Lewd are."

Lewis was standing with his arms akimbo. "This is nuts. How are you going to get this tree down to the driveway?"

"On your back," Alex said. "Any more wisecracks?"

Alex told Sid to back his car out of the driveway. He had intended to do the same with his van, but decided to nose it up against the garage in case he had to get tools from it. When that was done he had Lewis help him lay out some planks to roll the wagon along so the wheels wouldn't dig into the front lawn. At the step-down to the driveway he hung the planks about five feet out into mid-air. "When we get the tree to this spot we'll rig up the Come-Along so we can scoot the wagon out onto the planks and gradually ease it down. Mainly what I want you two to do is hang on to some ropes I'm going to tie to the tree."

Alex let the tree gently down onto the red Flyer. He secured it to the wagon the best he could, then he tied two ropes to the top of the tree. Lewis and Sid held on to the ropes while he took down the tripod and hooked the Come-Along to the post holding up the front porch. When at last he tried to move the wagon he found it rolled along a lot easier than he had expected. "What did I tell you," Sid said, straining at the end of his rope. "This is going to be a piece of cake."

"Don't be too optimistic. We have a long ways to go."

Alex rolled the wagon slowly along the planks while Lewis and Sid restrained the tree by pulling on the ropes. Each starboard step produced a pain that stabbed him in the groin.

"So what's with the limp?" Sid inquired, nodding down at Alex's foot.

"I hurt it."

"How?"

"In the line of duty." Alex felt this wasn't a lie as much as it was an extended metaphor for the mess he had got into since he first started working for Sid, and if he could possibly create a sense of blame in him it was for Sid's own good. At the gate, Alex realized there was going to be a problem. The branches reached out to touch the fence on either side, preventing it from going through.

"So now what do we do?" Lewis said.

"Now we get you to lift it," Alex told him.

"Screw off."

"Not until I get my wagon back, then I'll be glad to."

"So what *do* we do?" Sid asked him.

"I think we're going to play teeter-totter. Here, let's back up the wagon. I'll have to put some blocks under these planks."

Alex stacked concrete blocks under the planks, high enough to allow the lowest branches to srcape past the top of the fence. He tied a rope to the tree to restrain its descent once the wagon reached the summit directly over the fulcrum, then he attached the Come-Along opposite the rope and slowly winched the wagon and its cargo up the slope created by the planks. "Ingenious," Sid kept saying. "Bloody ingenious."

"I thought the expression was 'piece of cake'," Alex told him. "That too."

Alex secured the wagon with a rope so it wouldn't roll back down the planks. He removed the Come-Along and re-attached it to the post holding up the front porch, allowing enough slack in the cable for them to shove the wagon up over the crest. Very slowly the planks began to lift at one end and drop at the other. It took nearly forty-five minutes to get the wagon safely down to the driveway. When they got it to that point the going became a lot easier. There were no longer any obstacles between the tree and the hole, just a straight run on planks along the driveway and across the back yard.

"So can we dump it when we get to the hole?" Sid said, wrestling with his rope to keep the tree from swaying towards Lewis.

"No, I'm going to set up the tripod again."

"I don't see why we can't just shove the wagon over and let the tree slide in."

"Because it won't just slide in."

"I don't see why not."

Alex stopped the wagon. He put his foot against the right front wheel to keep it from rolling and stared at Sid. "Look, we got it this far, not because of your ingenuity but because of mine. Now let's just do it my way, okay?"

"Still, I don't see why we can't just dump it."

"First of all, it might ruin the wagon. Second of all, the tree would end up on its right side. Then I'll have a devil of a time getting it upright. Got it?"

Yarborough gave him a look that reminded him of a dog he had once punished with a rolled-up newspaper. While Sid and Lewis kept the tree from swaying, Alex picked up the planks the wagon had just rolled along and laid them in front of the ones the wagon was sitting on. He pulled the wagon forward. In another ten minutes they had reached the edge of the hole. "I think we could just tip it in," Yarborough told him.

"Look, just trust me," Alex said. "I know how to do this. Okay?"

Alex left Sid and Lewis with the single instruction to stand there and not let the tree waver, then went back to the front yard to get the two-by-fours that comprised the tripod. He had the boards on his shoulder and was heading to the back yard when he heard the tree come crashing down, limbs breaking on the ground. He dropped the two-by-fours and ran limping to the backyard where he found Sid and Lewis standing beside the overturned wagon which had spilled its cargo partly into the hole. Alex stood shaking his head, staring at the red Flyer whose wheels had folded over on one side, mangling the undercarriage and axels. "You just couldn't resist, could you? Now look at my kids' wagon. You ruined it."

"Yeah, but look at my tree. What about it?"

Where the tree had come down on the opposite rim of the hole the trunk had splintered in a compound fracture. "It looks like you'll have to make firewood out of it now," Alex sneered.

"Can't you just put a splint on it?"

Sid's suggestion made Alex want to slam him in the face, to pummel him with his fists until the man lay unconscious and bleeding. "Sure, just fix it, right? Just another little fix-it job for Alex, so some grownup brat can go on breaking his toys. Make it better, just make it all better. That's what you expect of me. That's all I'm kept around for . . . to fix up your toys so you can go on breaking them. Isn't that right, Sid? Isn't it? You're nothing but a spoiled brat, a brat who can stay a brat because he's got so much money. Well, to hell with you! To hell!"

Sid kept backing away, looking at him the way someone does a person who is dangerously deranged. It was the vulnerabilty and fear in Sid's eyes that made Alex shove him, and then shove him again, down into the hole with the tree. Yarborough rolled over once in the dirt. He clutched at the rim of the hole and pulled himself to his feet, obviously expecting Alex to swoop down on him. Lewis was in fast retreat, heading for safety somewhere around the house. Alex snatched up the twisted wagon and hurled it down at Yarborough and Yarborough, trying to jerk out of the way, fell backward over the tree and was cradled by its broken branches.

"That's where you belong, down in hell with your goddamn apple tree!" Alex bellowed, and lurched off towards the van, pain stabbing him all the way. Only when he backed the van out into the street and turned it around in the direction of home, did he experience that lightning bolt of realization about what he had just done. Suddenly the street beyond the windshield was transformed and he saw tumbling down from the boulevards on either side not just one apple tree, but legions of them, falling like dominoes back and forth across his path, in diminishing perspective that became a pinpoint far off in the future.

CADILLACS AND CHEVIES DON'T MIX

Maisey's Diner was located across the street from my dad's service station. It resembled a refurbished dining car side-tracked back in the 1940s. There were striped awnings over the windows and the main entrance, and sticking high above the roof was a topknot of glowing red neon. In the spring when the dust began to lift in the streets Maisey would hire me to wash down the windows and the front of the building, a job I performed about every two weeks.

Maisey was a short, heavy woman in her forties, with a bottom as big as a barrel. Her personality was what you thought of as expansive and good-natured but on occasion, if you caught her unaware, you could see her wring her hands and wince. Her husband Eugene worked in the kitchen slinging steaks and greasing fries. He was a good cook but he didn't like to meet the public and so he had married Maisey. "She's the best little public image I have," he once told me. "Without her my life wouldn't have any sauce."

One thing Maisey had set her mind on was trying to find my dad a good woman to marry. She didn't think it was right bringing up two boys in a garage, where, according to her, an unseemly sort of atmosphere prevailed. Sometimes she would stand on the stoop of the diner and jokingly curse my dad across the street at the garage. Usually she rounded out these tirades with threats of finding him a wife, at which he would wave his hand and disappear inside the bay.

My brother and I ate most of our meals over at the diner. Maisey served us what she called her specials, which were well-rounded meals at half the regular price. We could afford them at the menu price since we both worked in the garage, but Maisey wouldn't let us pay any more than half.

One day when I entered the diner, Maisey acted all fidgety and nervous. She spilled a milkshake on me and frantically mopped it up. There was one other customer in the diner at the time, a man I took to be a travelling salesman. When I saw him looking at her in the mirror I pretended I didn't care about the milkshake being spilled all over me, even though it had made my crotch look like a cherry sundae. "Don't bother," I said. "I'll go home to change."

Maisey wouldn't hear of it. "Eugene," she called. "I ruined this poor boy's clothes. Do you have some pants you can lend him while I wash these?"

"Tell him to go to the washroom. I'll pass them in to him."

I went into the washroom and came back wearing a floppy pair of trousers doubled up at the ankles. Eugene had kept my steak and fries warm in the kitchen and Maisey had made me another milkshake. She was still acting fidgety and I couldn't figure out why until she told me her sister was coming to visit her. "Her name's Marg and she needs someone to fall back on until she recovers from her divorce."

I filled my mouth with steak and fries so I wouldn't have to say anything. She was sitting across from me in the booth, her fat arms propping her chin. I chewed methodically and filled my mouth again. It was only about the tenth time she had tried to push a mom off on us and I always tried to let it slide so I wouldn't hurt her feelings.

"Marg is a nice woman. She has two lovely children, one a girl about your age. She cooks well and she keeps a clean house and I thought your dad might like to meet her."

"Well, gee, Maisey. I don't know, Maisey. He might and he might not. You know how my dad is about those things."

"Yes, I know how your dad is," she said. "He hides himself away in that garage just like Eugene does in the kitchen. Work, work, work, that's all he thinks of, while you boys gallivant from here to Kingdom Come."

"That's something you'll have to take up with my dad," I said. "I can't tell him who to meet or how to meet them."

"I know that," she said. "But Marg is a nice woman. I think he should at least have the opportunity to meet her."

My mom had died ten years before from a nervous ailment that had increasingly confined her to her bed and I knew my dad didn't want to go through that sort of thing again. Although he looked tough he was really very gentle and timid. He had limited his life to the garage and the customers who came in to have their cars repaired and that was the way he liked it. My brother and I had gotten used to not having a mom around and we didn't desire one that would mess up our lives by making us adhere to the principles of good hygiene and the like.

Usually, when Maisey set her mind on getting us a mom, my dad would decide to take a holiday and go fishing. This time was different, though. The mom in question was Maisey's sister and she had been invited to stay the month. While my dad wasn't broke he could not afford to take an extended holiday that might mean weeks away from the garage. Summer was the busiest time of year for us owing to the tourists that came through town and the loss of a week might mean as much as several thousand dollars in business. Of course, he could have left Tom and me in charge, but neither of us qualified as mechanics, even though Tom liked to think he was one.

Marg, as it turned out, was quite good looking. By that I mean she didn't look like a mom, especially not a mom with a fifteen-year-old daughter and a twelve-year-old son. She was slim and she kept her hair done in a loose roll at the back of her head that made her look like a cross between a librarian and one of those models you see in magazines. And her daughter was just the same, only younger.

The day they arrived my brother and I were standing in the station having a Coke. The brown LTD came down the street at a crawl and stopped in front of the diner and moments later Maisey came out to kiss and hug the occupants. My brother was an acute observer and the first thing he noticed were parts of the anatomy. "Wow-wee," he said, shaking his head. "Look at them points. How would you like to have those for a trophy?"

"She's too old for you," I said.

"Not the mom," Tom said. "The babe, the babe."

Tom shook his head and groaned.

"We've gotta get Dad married, just so I can be around them points. They really make my engine purr."

I looked at the girl. She was about five feet two inches, with dark hair that came down to her shoulders. Her face was kind of pert and her eyes contained that feverish look typical of girls her age.

"I'm not going into cahoots with you," I said. "You can move away when you want. But me, I have to live here. I don't want any secondhand mom telling me what to do."

"It's time you had a mom," Tom said. "Every young boy needs a mom. Otherwise they grow up screwy."

"Don't give me any of Maisey's crap," I said. "I don't want a mom."

"You'd have a little brother to play with," he said cutely. "Wouldn't you like that?"

"No, I wouldn't," I told him.

Tom was six feet tall. Occasionally I would come upon him flexing his muscles in front of the bathroom mirror. In high school he had been a halfback on the football team. Now he was waiting for fall to come, when he would trot off to university for four years. I was not about to let my position be jeopardized by him when he was only thinking of his momentary pleasure. A mom would make you brush your teeth before you left the house, she'd make you straighten your room and God knows what else.

I avoided the diner that evening but by noon the next day I was too hungry to stay away any longer. She wagged a finger at me. "Don't tell me you were too bashful to come by for supper last night?" she said.

"Naw, I was just busy. I grabbed a sandwich and took off."

Maisey admonished me for eating on the run. "You have to give your stomach time to digest. When you eat on the run you only frustrate it."

I shoved a piece of pork chop in my mouth, hotly pursuing it with a forkful of mashed potatoes and peas.

"I'm going to send Marg's son over to meet you," she said. "His name's Rob and I want you to make him feel at home. Would you do that for me?"

"I guess I can, only he has to meet me at Perrin's."

Perrin's drugstore was where everyone hung out. Rob arrived about one o'clock. He was what you typically thought of as a city boy. His clothes were nice and there wasn't any dirt on the knees of his trousers. I got the impression that he moped a lot because the first thing he spoke of was his dad. "But he's gone now," he said. "Mom made him go away."

"Where did he go?"

"Alaska."

"Why there?"

"I don't know. That's where Mom said he went."

I could see right away that Rob needed an education in small-town manners so I took him to the swamp to catch frogs. In the process of trying to catch one he fell in and got all muddy. I stopped his whining by throwing some mud at him. He was worried about what his mom would say so I told him to tell her he was a man and didn't have to give any excuses.

I liked Rob a lot better after we went to the swamp. For a city kid he was really too easy to fool. I would take him into Perrin's drugstore to buy lots of junk and get him to foot the bill. By the end of the week he was in the frame of mind where he would do almost anything, so I took him up to the dump to complete his education. At the dump I had a stash of girlie magazines. I told him what girls were all about and what a guy was supposed to do to them. He told me he was going to ask his mother if I was telling the truth, and I encouraged him to do so, thinking it wouldn't set too well with her.

On the following Friday, Eugene came over to see my dad about dropping by for the evening. "The kids can play parcheesi or something while we adults sit around talking."

"That's awful nice of you, Eugene." My dad was lying on a pushboard. His face was smudged with grease. "But you can see how busy I am. I'll probably be busy until way next June."

"I have it on the word of Maisey that she'll make a lot of trouble for you if you don't come. That means a lot of trouble for me."

My dad pushed himself back under the car and started clanking at something with a wrench. "You know how sorry I am about that, Eugene. But I can't afford to take a holiday."

"Do you want me to tell Maisey that?"

"I'm sure you can fix it with Maisey."

Eugene stood there in the bay wiping his hands on his apron, looking about as disconsolate as a fellow could be.

"George," he said, "You're not being fair about this. I come here regularly to have my car serviced and the least you could do is reciprocate by not causing me any trouble with my wife."

"Dammit, Eugene!" my dad said, pushing out from under the car. "A thing like this only means a little tiff for you but for me it means being pushed into familiarities I don't want to be pushed into."

"There are worse things."

"Sure, we could all be ploughed under," my dad said, "but that ain't nothing compared to being pushed into familiarities with a woman."

"George, you're not being reasonable. All I want you to do is come by for the evening. Then, like me, you can hide out until Marg is gone. That would be the manly thing to do because you'd be getting me off the hook too."

Dad was a great one for doing the manly thing. Once, because a woman couldn't afford to have her carburetor repaired, he did all the work for free, simply because she said her daughter was sick in Seattle and she had been on her way to see her. But something like that was nothing compared to the idea of maybe starting up a relationship.

"No, I'm sorry," he said. "I'm afraid I can't."

Eugene was testy. "Then let me put it this way," he said. "If you don't come you're going to have to deal with Maisey yourself."

"Dammit, Eugene!" my dad said. "You're out to inflict all sorts of pain on me. All I want to do is repair cars, that's all."

"And then there is our friendship to consider," Eugene went on. "How far back does it go? Twenty years. Twenty-five?"

"Dammit, Eugene. Cut it out."

"Then why don't you come over for the evening? I swear I'll make it as short as possible."

My dad dragged himself back under the car.

"Okay, Eugene. You win. You win."

My dad was not a sociable person, other than at business. He would drag himself home from work and toss himself down in the armchair and stare off into space while he played some marching music on the record player. After recuperating he would make himself a sandwich and read a while before going to bed. It was a simple routine he clung to almost savagely and if you didn't know him well you might have thought him stupid. But I knew he thought about Mother a lot, Mother and Death.

We closed the station early that evening. My brother had already made the aquaintance of Marg's daughter, Jill. He spoke of her in terms of wow and fantastic. "And those points," he said. "Those blessed, lovely points. They make my hands itch just thinking of them."

"You better keep your hands to yourself tonight," my dad said. "I want you two to be gentlemen. No wisecracks, no swearing. Nothing like that."

"Have you ever thought about getting married?" my brother asked.

"No, I haven't," he said. "Marriage is one thing I don't want and I advise you to keep your distance from it too."

"Jill's mother is sure good-looking," my brother said. "For someone her age, anyway."

"I wouldn't know," my dad said. "I haven't had time to notice her."

At eight o'clock, we were ready to go. I tagged along at the rear, feeling apprehensive about the evening. My brother kept tossing jokes at my dad, but my dad kept a gruff silence.

Maisey and Eugene's house was six blocks from ours. Eugene was sitting on the porch swing waiting for us. He was dressed in a shirt and tie and looked as miserable as a guy could be.

"I'm glad you could make it, George."

"I bet you are," my dad said sarcastically.

Eugene turned to glance at the windows. He threw back one of the pillows on the porch swing and took out a flask of whisky. "How about a drink from Jack Daniel's well?"

"I don't mind if I do." My dad tipped back the bottle and smacked his lips, whereupon he tipped back the bottle again.

"How about me?" my brother said.

My dad ignored him, passing the bottle back to Eugene. Eugene took a swig, then we went inside.

The evening came off a little too well. Jill and Rob and my brother and I played parcheesi in the front room while the adults drank beer and told jokes in the kitchen. I got the feeling that Dad had warmed up to Marg by the way he was talking and carrying on and that bothered me a little.

Maisey and Eugene's house was like a museum. It was full of relics that harked back to a previous era: over-stuffed furniture, knick-knacks from Niagara Falls, a crank telephone, a coffee-grinder, a gramaphone, things of that nature.

Jill and Tom kept taking short trips to other parts of the house. She would disappear and a little while later he would disappear. There would be a lot of giggling and Jill would reappear with a chafed face, closely pursued by my brother Tom.

"If you guys keep going off like that we're never going to finish this game," I said. "What's so interesting back there anyway?"

Jill would seat herself primly beside the parcheesi board and daintily pull at her skirt. "You'll understand when you're older," she said.

"I'm only a year behind you."

"In years," she said. "But in maturity you're ages behind, believe me."

When the parcheesi game was over Rob and I fooled around with the radio. There was a knob you could adjust to get different frequencies. Once we picked up what we thought was China and another time we picked up Sheriff Forbes saying he was going to have supper at Maisey's. "Hey, did you hear that?" I told my brother. "Forbes is going to Maisey's. Boy, is he in for a surprise!"

We waited by the radio for Sheriff Forbes to drive to the diner. About three minutes later his voice came on the air again. "This is me, Sid. I'm at the diner, only it seems to be closed. Do you remember Maisey saying anything about closing early?"

"No, I don't, Fred. She didn't say anything to me."

"That'strange. I think I'll swing around to her house to see if the lights are on."

At that, we went into action. I told Rob to go into the kitchen and stand by the light switch. Tom and Jill turned off the lights on the porch and I dimmed the ones in the hallway. Now only the lamp in the front room was on, and the globe in the kitchen. I glanced at Tom and Jill out at the gate. When Tom whistled that Sheriff Forbes was coming I turned out the front room light. That was Rob's cue to switch off the one in the kitchen.

Immediately the house plummeted into dark. There were shouts from Marg and Maisey to turn on the lights, but by then the cruiser had stopped in the street. I heard Jill yell for help, followed by my brother's voice: "Oh, come on, Jill. Just let me feel them."

"No, get your hands off me. Get them off," she said, her breath struggling out.

The ruse worked really well. Sheriff Forbes got out of the cruiser and came running up the front steps with his pistol drawn. "Halt! Stop there!" he yelled. "This is the police. We have the house surrounded."

In the kitchen, the light came on. Maisey and Eugene came running into the front room, followed by Marg and my dad. None of them looked very happy, especially my dad who had told us to be on our best behaviour.

"I'm sorry this happened, Sheriff. I don't know what got into the children." Maisey eyed me in particular. "But what can you expect of boys who don't have a mother?"

Tom and Jill had come in the back way. Jill's hair was messed around and Tom was grinning, ear to ear.

"What I want to know is how they knew I was coming by the house?" Sheriff Forbes said.

It was up to me to explain the part played by the radio. I gave a real bang-up account and in the end everybody was chuckling.

"He's a sweet boy," Maisey said, "but he's mischievous."

"I guess that's my fault," my dad said. "I don't keep a tight enough rein on them."

"Nor I," said Marg, glancing at her daughter.

When we got home it was nearly one o'clock. The incident of the radio had been glossed over and I was feeling pretty satisfied with myself.

Sundays were rather slow and lethargic. We opened the station late and closed early. Usually I had to work the shift from 2 p.m. to 5 p.m., although Dad would drop by just to see that everything was okay. That Sunday my brother had a date with Jill to go out in the countryside. He picked her up in front of the diner in his Chevy and headed off in the direction of the dunes. About thirty minutes later Marg came by the station in the LTD and asked me if I had seen her daughter and I told her she had had a date with Tom. She demanded that I phone my dad and I did and they drove off together in the LTD in the direction of the dunes.

Shortly after they left, my brother drove the Chevy into town from the opposite direction. He dumped Jill off at the diner, parked the Chevy at the station and ran back over to Maisey's where, through the window, I could see them each having a sundae. I figured this was pretty funny so I sat back with a Coke to see what developed. About forty-five minutes later the LTD screeched to a halt in front of Maisey's and my dad and Marg got out and stormed into the diner where I saw them standing at the end of the booth talking to Jill and Tom. At that point they all started looking out the window at the station and I figured I was in big trouble.

My dad had always taught me to stand my ground; however, the odds of four to one weren't my kind of odds, especially in the light of the trouble I had been making of late. I ran outside and hopped on my bike and pedalled away as fast as I could in the direction of the swamp. At the edge of town there is a steep hill you have to go down to get to the woods. I missed the trail going down and hurtled over the precipice and that was the last thing I remembered for a while.

When I woke I was lying in bed with an awful pain in my head and Maisey was sitting beside me in a chair. "Well, well, so you decided to come around," she smiled. "You're lucky I'm sitting here and not your father."

"Was he mad?"

"Do you know what a bull looks like when it sees red?"

"He was that mad?"

"Madder," she said. "So mad you might have driven him into getting married, my little rooster."

When I was fourteen I wasn't very wise about human nature. Through my various pranks I had hoped to show Marg what a lousy son I would make, but rather than doing that I had managed to confirm to Dad just how wild and undisciplined my brother and I had become. My dad was a slow, methodical thinker. He would dwell on something for days, turning it over and over as one did a stone to see every side of it. The conclusion he came up with was exactly what Maisey had been drumming into his head over the years, that without a mother to exert some control over us we would never amount to anything.

The day I had the accident marked a turning point in my dad's and Marg's relationship. They started stepping out evenings to go to the movies or sometimes a classy restaurant up in Spokane. I had become quite doleful about the prospect of them getting married. My appetite began to suffer and I didn't feel like doing anything. I didn't even feel like hanging out in front of Perrin's drugstore.

I wasn't the only one feeling depressed. One day Rob came

over to the station and kind of hung around the office, getting in the way. It didn't take a lot of insight to see that he was feeling just about as low as I was. In fact, the way he let his head and shoulders sag I figured he was just about to sink down in a corner and cry.

"What the hell's wrong with you?" I asked.

"I don't know. I just don't feel good."

"I bet you miss your dad?" I said. "I bet that's it, huh?"

Rob wrenched this crumpled-up letter out of his pocket. "He sent me this letter," he said. "Actually not to me, to my mom."

"What's it say?"

"He says he misses us. He'd like to patch things up and stuff like that, and how these baseball tickets are going to waste because he doesn't have me to take to the games."

"You mean they've got baseball in Alaska?"

"He didn't really go there. That's just what my mom said."

"I see." I kind of sidled over to him. "Mind if I have a look at that letter?"

"What for?"

"Well, you miss your dad, don't you?"

"Sure."

"Then maybe we should see if we can't get something worked out. Here, give me the letter."

I quickly read the letter, and God, was it depressing. Rob's dad was even more depressed than Rob and I put together, and a helluva lot more sappy about it. But that letter was all I needed to get my enthusiasm back. I told Rob to meet me later in the afternoon. Together we composed this letter saying how Rob thought his mother was feeling pretty sad about things, and how she might be thinking of getting back together, too, but that this was all on the q.t. and shouldn't be related to his mother who kept talking about committing suicide and stuff like that. We dropped that letter off at the post office, and by the first of the week Rob's dad had arrived in town in his Cadillac.

Cadillac drivers are generally of three types: poor Cadillac drivers who buy a couple gallons of gas in order to get themselves maybe sixteen miles from where they are; credit-card Cadillac drivers who wheel around a company car at the company's expense; and rich Cadillac drivers who don't give a shit how much they spend getting to where they're going. Rob's dad fit the second category. He drove a company car at the company's expense because of a job he held down in advertising.

At forty-six, my dad was a tall lean man with dark curly hair and eyes inset below a rugged brow. Five years before, he had had an accident that put him in the hospital with two broken legs and a split pelvis. He had been working under a car when the jack failed and the weight of the vehicle came down on him. The doctors at the hospital had told him he might never walk again, but by eight months he was back on his feet, and by twelve months he was working in the garage.

Rob's dad was a tall muscular man who was beginning to go to flesh. I could see by his complexion that he drank a lot and didn't work it out of his system with enough exercise. But in a flashy, tailor-made suit, he was able to look like a vigorous man. And he didn't have grease under his fingernails.

Though I thought my dad the better man I was willing to concede the race to Rob's dad. I figured he had laid claim to Marg first and by rights he should be allowed to keep her, and I was willing to do my best to help him.

Rob's dad got a room at the hotel. The next day he went to see Rob's mom. Marg and he had a fight and he returned to the hotel, after a brief stop-over at the bar. The next day Jill and Rob went to see him. Then it was my turn.

Rob's dad listened very patiently to my proposal. Occasionally he would nod or heave a sigh and I would hurry on to the next point. When I was through, he said, "You've told me everything except why you're doing this."

"Well, it's like this, sir. I've been without a mom for over ten years. Ten years is a long time in a guy's life. You get used to a certain way of living."

"You mean you'd prefer not to have a mother?"

"That's right. A mom would only mess things up. She'd tell me what to do and things like that. But I don't need to be told what to do. I'm my own man, and I like it that way. I don't think Marg could adjust to that."

He gave a laugh. "You know, I think you've hit the nail on the head."

We sealed our agreement with a handshake, then I went to see Rob's mom. Rob's mom was rather cool toward me. I explained the same thing to her that I had to her former husband, only I souped it up a little.

"What makes you think your dad and I wouldn't be compatible?"

"Well, for one thing, he can't get my mom off his mind. Like last night. I caught him looking at her picture. You know, really looking at it. Then this morning he told me to phone the florist for some flowers to put on her grave."

She stared at me through the smoke of her cigarette and I could see she was trying to figure out how much I was lying. "It's like that all the time," I said. "He loved her a lot, and so did I."

"You don't think I could replace her. Is that what you're trying to say?"

"Yeah, I guess that's what I'm trying to say."

I left her sitting in Maisey's front room and went to the station. That night Dad was scheduled to go out with her. I stayed upstairs in my room playing with the crystal radio I had made out of a spool of wire, a razor blade and the lead of a pencil. I had won the earphones in a game of mumbly peg at school and I had gotten the instructions for the radio out of a library book. Earlier that evening my brother had gone to Spokane to get his ashes sifted. It was a cool night, and except for some mice that were holding a track meet in the ceiling, the house was pretty quiet.

It was two o'clock when Dad got home. He was singing loudly in a drunkard's voice. I climbed out of bed and went downstairs where I found him holding up a record to the light in order to read the label. When he found the record he wanted, he put it on the turntable, sat down in the armchair and put his feet up on the hassock. The record player blared a marching number that he conducted with his hands.

About that time my brother dragged himself into the house. Tom looked like a steamroller had run over him. He flopped down on the sofa and stared at Dad. "I take it your night went all right," he said.

Dad kept waving his hands to the music, apparently oblivious to him.

"Remind me never to mess around with those Spokane whores ever again," my brother went on. "Dick and I went up there tonight and, boy, I tell you they made me numb."

I was listening, but Dad didn't seem to be. He kept waving his hands to the music.

"Actually they weren't whores, I guess. Just a couple of sluts we picked up, but Christ . . ."

"I don't want to hear about it," my dad said. "Whatever you pick up is your own business, and that includes the syph."

The music stopped and my dad went to put on another record.

"Well, how did your night go?" my brother tried again.

"I'm afraid I failed," my dad said. "She wouldn't have me. I popped the question, but she wouldn't have me."

"Why?"

My dad gave me a shrewd glance. "Let's just say she decided not to after the facts were explained to her."

"What facts?"

"Just the facts."

A few days later Maisey's sister left town, followed by her husband in the Cadillac. I went over to say goodbye to Rob, but Dad was too busy under a car to say goodbye to Marg.

It was good to have things back the way they had been.

THE VIOLENT LAVENDER BEAST

This, then, was how it happened: how Antone Perry, one unequivocal morning, came to run with the hounds. Unlike other mornings, darkness withdrew and left behind in its wake a lavender sky, and his wife, who had quarrelled with him the previous evening — in front of the children, the islanders and, quite possibly, God Himself — awoke to find a note, scrawled on a torn piece of brown paper bag, pinned by a hunting knife to the pillow beside her head. The sky behind Shaggy Hill was so radiant it looked as if a volcano had erupted, spewing lavender all over the heavens. Down in the meadow, where a wheelbarrow lay rusting on its side, the colour was thrown back by each droplet of dew bending the tall grass. Only the mist which swirled and eddied was indifferent to it, hovering as grey as gossamer in the cold air. Lying in bed, swaddled by warm blankets, Yvonne imagined the hounds slithering off into the wooded gloom, followed by Antone, down on all fours, switching his buttocks as the shadows took him in.

Clothes were heaped on the burnpile and the smell of death had gone. The note, written in green crayon, was stuck to the pillow that held Antone's head while he was sleeping off his drunken torpor on the living room floor. He had left the back door ajar and the house had cooled to the temperature outside and Yvonne, girdled by blankets up to her neck, watched her breath turn to fog above the note, which so far she had declined to read. A howl unwound like a bright ribbon through the deadfall on Shaggy Hill, one long piercing wail that eventually became lost in the gloom. The swaths of low-lying mist shifted uncertainly in the meadow, one of them recovering from the trailing vortex of the man who had recently passed through it. The house, although silent, echoed with shouting. The children were curled beneath their bedclothes, oblivious to the arrival of dawn. No matter how hard Yvonne tried to shake off the impression, she could not help but think of them as rats curled against the cold. The smell of death, which she and the girls lived with for almost a week, was gone now, and Antone had reverted to his animal self.

In the bedroom at the back of the house, bedsprings recoiled as Michelle, sound asleep, thrashed in the covers which had tangled round her limbs. Small quakes travelled through the floor and up the walls, jostling the trestle-like structure which Antone had built to hold her toys and books and drawing materials. Suddenly a volume dislodged, falling with a flutter of pages to the floor. Down by the pond the white geese, lying with beaks under their wings, unveiled stark eyes, staring off in the direction of the house. Earlier a man in T-shirt and jeans had stumbled down through the tall grass of the meadow, heading off into the shadow-laden depths of the woods. The clothes in the burnpile smoldered; rivulets of smoke trickled up from the charred remains, eventually to flow together into a greyish column. Yvonne felt the chill at the back of her neck and knew she must rise to start a fire in the cookstove. She snaked her arm through the folds of the bedclothes, up towards the pillow where the note was skewered by the hunting knife. She found she was empty of any emotion, carved out as she had been by yesterday's anger. In the adjacent bedroom her daughter Sylvia lay immersed in a dream. She was dancing, pirouetting across a field in the sunshine, towards a darkness that drew her as powerfully as a magnet. The hounds moved like stealthy shadows, wending their way through the dark underbrush, and Antone, feeling the sting of wet branches against his bare arms, suddenly stopped beside a stump, waiting for a sound — the breaking of a twig or the rustling of salal leaves — to guide him.

In the cold sod the rats lay curled against death. Mist swayed in the meadow, while out on the road the first of several cars roared by, heading in the direction of the ferry terminal. Yvonne pulled the hunting knife out of the pillow and dragged the note off the blade. The previous morning had been so different; Antone, having awakened early, had brought her steaming coffee in bed. He had planted a kiss between her breasts, in a mood of jovial rapport. The house had been warm — not cold like this morning, with her breath turning to fog each time she exhaled. Now another car went by the house, the sound of a hurtling wave of air that seemed to drive the chill deeper into her bones.

Dew ran together on the alder leaves, collecting in drops that plunged toward the surface of the pond. A raven flew out of the fold between Shaggy Hill and Heck Hill and, with low, guttural cries that resonated like dark laughter, it coursed down the glen. The note, scrawled in green crayon, said: *It's no good. Everything's gone to rot, rot and decay. And death. Antone.* Yvonne crumpled the note and hurled it in the corner beyond the mound of clothes draped in disarray on the ironing board. When she and the girls had come home from church the previous day, Antone had been raving drunk and everything they had kept in the basement was strewn in the side yard.

"God, is this what I come home to — filth, goddamn filth! Can't you keep anything clean?"

Sylvia's alarm clock sent its cheap rattle through the house. There came through the closet wall the sound of something being knocked over as her daughter sought to stifle the noise. Yvonne flung back the bedclothes and sat up. The floor was cold and already she could feel the cold ascending her legs. The previous night she had gone to bed with her sweater on, having cast a backward glance at Antone lying face down on the floor, gurgling through his nose and mouth each time he breathed. She remembered the glance he had given her down at the ferry terminal; it had been like a flash of blue steel from the corner of his eye.

"Smell — what smell?" he had said, tossing his blue duffel bag into the backseat of the car.

It had been his eyes which had alerted her. She hunched at the steering wheel and directed her gaze out the windshield. Foot passengers were finding their rides, others were pulling carts up the steep grade from the ferry terminal.

"I just wanted to warn you."

"Warn me?"

"About the smell."

"Listen, I don't want to hear about smells, not the first thing I get home."

The rattling of the clock had ceased, to be replaced by rock n' roll on Sylvia's radio. Yvonne, pulling on jeans, yelled at her through the closet wall: "Turn that thing down. Turn it down, right now."

Down by the pond, a white goose stretched its leg out behind it, the webbed toes spreading, then folding as it tucked its leg. A rabbit, seeing light go on inside the house, nosed its food tin towards the door of the hutch and a rat, searching for spilled pellets in the straw and manure, darted off into some nearby blackberry vines.

"Can't you see you've made a perfect place for them to breed? Can't you see that?" he had said, kicking a tea crate full of linen down the slope.

Drops beat a tattoo on the pond and the sky, suffused with lavender, seemed to swirl. Antone stood absolutely still in the dark forest. He thought he saw the hounds moving off through tangled deadfall on the hillside. He raised his ear in that direction, listening. Out on the highway another car sped past. Sylvia, lying in that half-conscious state between sleeping and waking, thought at first she was dreaming. She seemed to be floating in a void, watching her hands tape cardboard over a broken windowpane. Yvonne nudged her feet into slippers and headed through the living room towards the kitchen. She noticed the back door had been left open and cursed Antone under her breath. The lowest of the three panes had been masked by cardboard. She glanced at the hill which slouched like a shaggy beast. Antone was up there; he had awakened to barking in his head and had gone to run with the hounds—hounds he had convinced himself were roaming the hill. She switched on the kitchen light. The blue ceramic tiles inset in the ebony table formed a pool upon which a single white plate had set sail. Each time Yvonne picked him up at the terminal he smelled faintly of diesel from working around engines on the tugboats. Usually the first thing he did when he got home was take a bath. But on sniffing the air he had flung the duffel bag on the sofa and had gone downstairs to see if he could locate the odour.

"God, can't you tell when something's dead? That's the smell of death, Yvonne. Death."

Yvonne wadded sheets of newspaper and shoved them in the firebox of the cookstove. She latticed kindling on top of the paper, replaced the stoveplate at the rear and reached for the matchbox on the window sill above the sink. She struck a match and dropped it on the newspaper. Flames leaped through the stovehole at the front, carrying up a thin veil of smoke. For a moment she was held, entranced. The newspaper wrinkled, the kindling began to snap. With a rough clank, she replaced the nearest stoveplate. Again she heard the howl: high, sustained, gliding down from the hill and lodging near her heart.

When he had opened the basement door, the smell had washed over him: putrid, nauseating, pushing out with the warm air. He flung the door wide and stepped back to let the basement breathe. The house was old, riddled by decay and rat-holes. Immediately inside the door was a cistern covered by planks. In winter, a freshet ran across the floor, downhill towards the pond at the back of the property. His intention was to demolish the house and build anew, but his plans kept collapsing, folding back into dark oblivion. He reached around the door jamb and switched on the light. The airtight furnace sucked rhythmically at the air. The heat was caught by a canopy and funneled upstairs, along with the stench. Cobwebs hung from the beams and joists, lulling like waves on a peaceful bay. Whoever had last fed the rabbits had left the lid off the feed bucket on the table. Several feet away, lying partly under an old wringer washer, he saw a dead rat teeming with maggots.

"Jesus Christ, what do you do: come down here with blinders on?"

Rats peered out from the blackberry vines, waiting to see if the light in the house would be followed by somebody coming outside. When no one appeared, first one rat, and then another, scampered across the open ground to the manure pile beneath the hutches. The rabbits huddled in various corners of the cages, watching the rats dart like shadows across the mounds. Michelle awoke humming to herself. Light from the kitchen filtered through the curtain over the doorway. She could hear her sister's radio, her mother clanking the stoveplates. Antone climbed onto a large boulder. Squatting there, with his hands dangling between his thighs, he looked up the hill to where the lavender sky shone through the dark trees. The hounds were nowhere to be seen, but he thought he could hear them, panting up the slope, maybe fifty feet ahead of him.

"Where is the shovel, for shitsake? Why can't anyone put the tools back where they belong?"

Yvonne had heard him downstairs, roughly hurling things aside, cursing at the top of his voice. The girls had come from Sylvia's room where they had been watching television. They stood beside the vent in the floor, their faces pale and frozen.

"I take it Dad's home," Sylvia had said, scowling down at the vent.

"I think you girls better go to your rooms."

Then, from below the floor, in a voice that shook with rage: "God, there's another one, in the trough behind the deep freeze. I told you when I set out the poison to start looking for dead rats. Why didn't you?"

"Rats?" Michelle said, widening her eyes.

"Go to your rooms, and turn off the television. Quickly please."

"And here's another one, in a box of linen. No wonder it fucking stinks."

Sylvia felt herself being shaken.

"Come on, it's school today. Time to get up."

Sylvia could see through her eyelids that the light had come on in her room. She rolled over, dragging blankets over her head.

Her mother had shoved Antone back against the washing machine, shouting: "We don't need your help. You've done enough already."

In his drunkenness he had fallen off balance, sliding down the side of the machine. Sylvia blinked her eyes, trying not to remember. Yvonne shook her roughly by the shoulder. "What's the point in setting your alarm if I have to come in here and get you up every single morning? Can you tell me that? Can you?"

"I'm awake."

"Then get up. It's almost eight o'clock."

Yvonne switched off her daughter's radio and returned to the kitchen. In the dim light of the basement there had been too many shadows to see into every corner. He knew there must be more rats but where they had crawled off to die was impossible to tell. He grabbed the pail of dead ones and took it down to the meadow where he buried them beneath the sod. It was twilight and every window in the house was ablaze. He left the shovel and pail in the meadow and stalked back up to the house. He wedged the basement door so it would stay open and, with a face twisted by the putrid stench, he trudged up the back stairs, jarring open the rear door with a rough shove of his shoulder.

"Put something over the vent."

His face was a burl and Yvonne could tell he was extemely disgusted. "Did you get them all?"

"Some of them. I'll look for the rest tomorrow."

"I know you're mad at me," she said.

"I don't want to talk about it," he said. "I think I'll take a bath. My skin feels like it's crawling with maggots."

Michelle was humming, blinking her eyes. The lavender colour poured through the window onto her bedspread. When she opened her eyes her head seemed to fill with the pale purple, when she closed them the humming rose in pitch, seeming to vibrate throughout her body. Down by the pond one of the geese pushed itself to its feet and began to beat the the air with its wings. The fog stirred. Beyond the hill the sun struggled to rise through the mist. The hour of singing birds had gone. Usually the prattling would wake Yvonne and she would lie listening to it, alone in bed. Antone had risen from where he had slid to the floor. Leaning aginst the machine for support, he had kicked out the lower pane in the back door.

"Don't think you can lock me in here. No one locks me in. No one."

"Just leave, Antone. Go run with your bloody hounds. But leave us alone."

"I want to show you . . ."

"You showed me already. You don't need to show me again."

Sylvia threw back her blankets. She stared at the various photographs pinned to the wall, not really seeing the rock stars who peered back at her with mannequin faces. She and her mother had retreated down the back stairs, away from Antone's face in the broken pane, out to the side yard where their possessions were strewn on the lawn in the sun. What impressed her was how still the world had become: the trees, the sky, the meadow, they were silent, swayed by different currents.

When he came out of the bathroom his dark hair was plastered sleekly to his skull. A towel was draped around his waist, hanging to the level of his knees. He glanced at her by the kitchen sink and padded on bare feet towards the bedroom. Yvonne followed him to the doorway, watched the muscles writhe in his back.

"Would you like dinner now?"

"No, it'd make me puke."

"Well, I'm sorry. Sorry for living."

He turned outside the bedroom door. "I don't understand it. How could you live with that smell? Doesn't it make you want to vomit?"

"I didn't know what it was."

"Well, why didn't you try to track it down?"

Yvonne shrugged. "I thought it was the septic tank. Backing up."

"God, I can't believe it. I simply can't believe it."

"Look, I'm not like you. I didn't grow up in the country. I didn't learn about these sort of things."

"Come on, it's not that difficult. There's an obnoxious smell. You track it down. You don't just leave it, hoping it'll go away."

All week they had been burning incense and spraying with

Lysol, but Yvonne didn't tell him that. She didn't tell him she had feared the smell, that it had been so repugnant she had dreaded what she might find if she followed it to its source, down in the murky basement, where things rotted in dark corners, furtively, without being noticed.

Antone had brought her coffee in bed. He had planted a kiss between her breasts and had scooted off down the hall to the kitchen where he and Michelle were making pancakes for breakfast. When he came back to the bedroom to pour her a second cup of coffee she could tell by his preciseness, by the way he held himself so erect, that he had had something to drink. By breakfast his eyes had glazed over and rather than sitting down at the table beside her he had elected to continue making pancakes at the griddle.

"Drunk already," she had said, when she got up to put her plate in the sink.

He winked.

"In preparation of going down there," he said, bobbing his thumb at the floor. "I don't expect it's going to be very pleasant."

"I'm sure you'll see to that."

Down the glen came the guttural cry of a raven. Even in the house, lying in bed, Michelle could hear the wings fanning the air. She leaned towards the window, cocking her head and glancing askew at the sky. Above the trees on Shaggy Hill the mist swirled, now gathering together in a sort of mask, now becoming a lion's face with a great open maw. The previous day, when they had come home from church to find their things strewn in the side yard, her father had been so drunk on home brew he seemed to stumble with each move, a large raven that squawked and lurched.

"That smell you've been plagued with all week. You want to see what makes it?"

"You already told us," Yvonne said. "I don't think we need to see."

"I think you do."

"Really, Antone. Why do you get like this?"

"Look, I'm away for two weeks. I come home and the place reeks of death. And who has to clean it up? Me, always me."

The three of them—Yvonne, Sylvia and Michelle—had stood there in their good clothes, in a patch of sunlight on the lawn. A breeze caught the green ribbon in Michelle's blond hair, twisting it so that it took the light. Antone grabbed the garden rake. He hooked the prongs in one of Sylvia's old winter coats and dragged the garment over to them.

"This is where the smell comes from," he said, flipping back one half of the coat.

In the fold of the garment, the rats lay side by side, curled against death, teeming with maggots. The rank smell seemed to blossom around them.

"And that's only two of them. There's at least a half-dozen more in the same condition. That's why I'm always telling you to keep things clean, especially if you're going to raise animals."

"I try to keep them clean," Yvonne had said.

"What do you mean? The basement was filthy. Junk all over, mildewing. Scraps of food where the kids had their hideout. Don't tell me you were trying to keep things clean."

"Listen, I've been busy."

"Busy doing what, for godsake? I come home and all I do is catch you up on chores you haven't done."

Yvonne shoved a couple sticks into the firebox and clanked down the burner plate. Sylvia stumbled from her room, grinding the knuckles of her right hand around in her eyesocket. For a nightgown she was wearing Antone's red undershirt, the one that said Hawaii '84.

"Why's it so cold this morning?" she said, flicking on the bathroom light.

"Your father left the back door open."

"Where is he anyway?"

"Up on the hill," Yvonne told her, jerking her head in its direction.

Antone cupped his hands to his mouth, and howled. He listened for a reciprocating cry from the hounds but none came. The forest was perfectly quiet. Impelled by the thought that he might have lost them, he began to run up the slope, flailing his arms, driving himself through the underbrush. He had awakened on the living room floor, dreaming he was bent over the stern of the tugboat, examining the froth produced by the slowly spinning propeller, when suddenly this pallid blob rolled up out of the water. It was swollen, breaking apart. At first he thought it was a jellyfish, then he saw the lipless mouth and the teeth arrayed like coral, and he knew he was remembering.

"Select what you want, and the rest goes down to the burnpile."

"We'll haul it all down there," Yvonne shouted, scraping light brown hair away from her eyes. "We'll burn it all."

"You don't have to burn it all. Just the stuff that's garbage."

"Well, isn't it all garbage—according to you!"

Michelle watched the lavender face swirl off over the tops of the trees. In the kitchen she heard the refrigerator door being closed. "Is it breakfast yet?"

"Not yet, dear."

"Should I get up?"

"Why don't you wait until the house gets warm. It's still pretty cold."

In the dark of the bedroom, he had lain perfectly still, his body depressing the other half of the mattress, faintly smelling of diesel despite having taken a bath.

"Look, I'm sorry. I should've found the rats myself."

"Forget it. I don't want to think about it."

"I should've, though. I know you told me to."

"Listen, I'm tired. I haven't slept in over thirty-six hours. My mind is reeling. I can hardly keep it together, I want to go to sleep."

Soon he was snoring, like a mechanical bellows, each expiration seeming to fill the darkness with the taint of diesel. She turned her head to look at him, saw a vague outline of his profile. He seemed a smoldering mound in the dark, and any second she expected him to burst into flames. Lifting the covers, she gently rolled out of bed. Late into the night she sat in the rocking chair beside the lamp, alternately reading and watching the rivulet of smoke drift up from the stick of incense.

Sylvia wiped herself with tissue paper and flushed the toilet. Washing her hands at the sink, admiring herself in the mirror, she suddenly remembered her father sitting in the folding chair, his feet up on the rail of the deck, drinking home brew from a large Coke bottle, as they hauled things down to the burnpile. Once he had leaned back so far to gulp down the contents of the bottle, the chair toppled backwards, spilling him onto the deck. He bounced back up like a human rubber ball, cursing and kicking the chair.

"I guess you know what sort of example you're setting," Yvonne told him, walking back up the slope from the burnpile.

"I'm sure you'll keep me informed."

Just then, a car slowed out on the road, a Toyota station wagon. The round pink face of the minister peered from the open window on the driver's side. "Having a yardsale?"

Yvonne forced a smile. "A fall clean-up."

"I didn't get a chance to say how much we enjoyed Sylvia's solo this morning. She sang like an angel, an absolute angel."

Sylvia slid back the bathroom door and switched off the light. Yvonne was standing at the cookstove, laying strips of bacon in a skillet. Even from a distance, Sylvia could see she was crying, silently, without the slightest spasm. Antone had stumbled down the stairs from the deck and had ducked through the basement door, and Yvonne knew he was headed toward the shelf where he kept the Coke bottles of home brew. The minister, noticing Antone's unstable condition, had tipped his hand to his mouth. Yvonne nodded. The minister mouthed the phrase, "Is there anything I can do?"

Yvonne shook her head.

"Don't neglect to call if you need my help," the minster said, smiling.

"I won't."

Sylvia trudged up the slope from the burnpile, her hands tucked into the sleeves of her sweat shirt. The minister said, "Ah, here she is now. I just stopped by to say how much we enjoyed your solo. It really brightened the service."

Antone was standing back in the doorway, a bottle hanging from his right hand, mouthing the minister's phrase in a mocking sort of way. He uncapped the bottle with the aid of his belt buckle and foam spewed from the neck, running down over his jeans.

"Thank you for the kind words," Yvonne said. "We had better get back to work, though."

"Yes, we've got rats," Michelle said. "Lots of dead rats. Everywhere."

"Rats," the minister said.

"Yes, my dad poisoned them and now they're all dead."

"Well, I'll leave you to it then," the minister said.

Sylvia stood at the mirror, offering up her breasts to her reflection, dreaming of the man she would one day give herself to. He would be tall. He would buy her things: beautiful clothes, jewelry. He would take her to places far away. And he wouldn't get raving drunk. Yvonne broke eggs into the stainless steel bowl and beat them with the whisk. Through the window she could see the lavender sky beginning to dilute, as the sun rose steadily higher beyond Shaggy Hill. In a few minutes the bright aura would become a fiery disk; the sunshine would slant through the windows, warming the house. The large brown stud-rabbit nosed its water dish round the inside of the hutch. Several geese had drifted out onto the pond where drops beat a tattoo on the surface. Antone had lost track of the hounds. He trudged with heavy steps up the hillside, now recalling what he had left below. He remembered the canvas he had attempted to paint, the one depicting the lipless, toothy corpse in the lower left, himself leaning over the stern of the tug, staring into the face of death, while arrayed in the background were scenes from domestica, a carnival, a town with a cathedral, sushine spilling down through the thunder clouds — it had all gone to rot. Everything. There were no more spangled days. Only a vague sort of unrelenting misery, and duties performed without savour.

Michelle called from her bedroom. "I'm tired of being asleep. Can I get up and colour?"

"Only if you put your slippers on. And a sweater."

"Red's looking in the window. Can I let him in?"

"If you keep him in your room. I don't want him underfoot in the kitchen."

Michelle pulled on a sweater and scooted her feet into slippers.

She traipsed to the back door and let in the orange tabby. "Mom, he's been hunting again."

"How can you tell?"

"His feet are all wet, like he's been in the field."

Yvonne felt her eyebrows lift. She flipped the bacon in the skillet, remembering how Antone had suddenly jolted to his feet, clutching the deck rail and listening off up the hill. "There, can you hear them? They're roaming the hill, four of them, each howling in turn."

"You're drunk, Antone."

But he didn't hear her, so transfixed was he by the howling in his head. Later, he vomited over the side of the deck, then, stumbling and weaving, he went into the house, only to come back outside in his running togs. Clinging to the rail so he wouldn't fall down the steps, he managed to descend to the ground and jog off towards the gate. "See you in a while. I'm going to run around the island."

"You'll kill yourself, Antone."

"If I do you can bury me with the rats."

Michelle put the orange tabby on the shelf above her drawing table and told him to stay put. He tried to scamper off down the length of the activity trestle, but Michelle brought him back and told him to sit. "If you don't I'll have to do something," she said, wagging her finger at him. The cat got up and began to meander off down the shelf in the direction of the kitchen. Michelle went to the dresser and pulled back the drawer where she kept the treats. She held the treats up to Red's nose and lured him back to where she wanted him to sit, feeding him a treat whenever he became restive.

"Now I'm going to draw you. So don't move. And smile, like so," she said, molding his face into a smile that revealed his needle teeth. Red swiped at her hand and she gave him another treat. "What colour do you want to be? Black or maybe green? How about purple? That's a good colour for you."

Yvonne poured off the grease and put the skillet back on the cookstove. She poured the eggs from the stainless steel bowl and called out towards the bedrooms. "Breakfast is almost on the table. I hope you're dressed and ready to eat."

"Almost," Sylvia responded.

Yvonne took three plates out of the cupboard and set them on the stove to warm. The fire was burning too fast. She dampered it until a trickle of smoke appeared at one of the stoveplates, then gave it more air. When they finished carting things down to the burnpile, she swept up the glass from the broken pane and told Sylvia to tape cardboard over the opening while she made them a late lunch. She wasn't thinking; she was moving through a thick medium, a sort of translucent gel, mindless, carved out inside. Ever since Antone had stopped painting he had been impossible to live with. The only time he seemed the least bit happy was when he sat with Michelle at her drawing table, showing her how to achieve certain effects on paper. The rest of the time he cursed his life.

Antone reached the top of the hill. He looked off across the lowlands where mist was rising in a thick, steamy veil before the platinum disk of the sun. It was too bright to keep looking in that direction. He shaded his eyes with his hand. Then he turned with a jerk, thinking he heard the hounds behind him, growling. Sylvia heard the howl: it spiralled down from Shaggy Hill, and for a moment, she was stricken by it. She remembered her father returning from his run, sweating, his face and chest bleeding from lacerations where gravel still clung, his mouth twisted in a clownish smile.

"I made it around the island. I guess I'm supposed to live after all."

Yvonne had turned and stalked out of the room. Antone had followed her.

"No, get away from me. Don't even try to talk."

"What did I do?"

"Take a look at the window in the back door, then you figure it out, you fool, you drunken fool. You come waltzing in here like nothing has happened, like you haven't made life hell for us. Get out of my sight. I hate you."

When he threw the match on the gasoline-soaked rags the sudden heat made him rear back. His nostrils filled with the scent of his singed eyebrows and hair, and he swiped at them to make sure he hadn't caught fire. The flames quickly devoured the things on top of the burnpile, and settled down to gnaw their way through the rest of the junk. A plastic doll's head puffed like a marshmallow, then melted in around the glass eyeballs, which finally dropped out of sight into the burning. He poked at the pile with a rake, periodically guzzling from the large Coke bottle that leaned on its side in the tall grass. The white geese honked at the fire from a safe distance, running their necks along the ground and bringing up their heads to hiss. Antone tossed a burning rubber boot at them and the geese attacked it, only to pull back with outraged squawks.

Yvonne scraped a spoon around the inside of the skillet, folding the cooked eggs back into the runny ones. "Hold still," Michelle told the cat. "I can't draw you if you keep moving around." What had begun as a portrait of Red, had evolved into something else; the needle teeth dominated, the face seemed that of a mythical beast, one that swirled into existence out of the background colors. "You know, I can't get you the way you should be if you don't behave. You're going to be different than you are."

When he entered the house he brought with him the smell of burning. His eyebrows were singed off and the exposed flesh gave him a stark look. Yvonne was sitting in a chair beside the dark window. She had chased the girls into their bedrooms, not to go to sleep, but to stay out of sight. She glowered at him in silence, her face a livid mask. Though he was drunk, it was the drunkeness of a somber man, one who oozed defeat. She watched him cross the living room floor to the bedroom and switch on the light.

"I hope you're not intending to go to sleep like that," she said.

"I'm just getting some clean clothes. Is that all right?"

"Don't linger in there. I don't want you stinking up the room."

"Listen to who's complaining about stink. Someone who can't even smell death seeping up through the floor."

He took clean clothes to the bathroom. She heard him splashing in the tub, then everything was silent, except for the mechanical trills and hums, that of the refrigerator and the clock on the kitchen wall.

"Mom, I have to go pee," Michelle said.

"Well, you'll just have to wait until your father gets out of the bathroom."

"I can't wait any longer."

"Then knock on the door and see if he'll let you in."

Yvonne heard Michelle tap on the door. Heard her pad back out to the living room. "He doesn't answer."

"For godsake," Yvonne said, rising from the chair and heading to the bathroom. She knocked loudly on the door. "Michelle has to go to the bathroom. Can she come in?"

There was no sound. She tried the door and found it unlocked. Antone had fallen asleep in the tub. His chin rested in the water and his heavy breathing made ripples on the surface. His legs were splayed, his pale knees poking up like great knobs. One hand was gripping his genitals.

"It's all right, dear. Just go right in."

Michelle sat on the toilet, looking at her father, in particular the hand which clutched his private parts.

"Why's he so still?"

"Because he's dead drunk. Too drunk to wake up and get out of the tub. Don't look at him. He's repulsive."

Antone's head had dropped so low in the water his breath was gurgling. Yvonne pulled the plug so the water would drain and then closed the door. Nearly half an hour later, she heard him banging around in the bathroom, swearing because he couldn't find a fresh towel. She went to the bedroom. Pretended to be reading. Finally he appeared at the doorway.

"Don't think you're going to sleep in here," she told him. "There's a pillow and a blanket on the floor. You can sleep out there."

"Maybe we should talk."

"Don't bother. You don't remember anything when you're drunk."

She heard him milling around in the kitchen, fixing himself something to eat. For a long time she lay in the dark, wrapped up in the warm blankets, unable to roll over into the arms of sleep. When she got up to go to the bathroom, she saw him conked out on the living room floor, drool hanging from his lips. And she envied his drunken sleep, his total oblivion.

Their eyes were small bright fires in the folds of their faces. They danced and lunged around him, clicking their teeth. He felt their fangs graze his forearms, like wooshes of air passing over his skin. He was thirteen and alone on the highway, delivering newspapers. Across the field, some crows took to the air. Everything beyond the yapping periphery of the dogs seemed so quiet, so still. For a moment, he understood his mortality, then he felt a weakness in his bowels, followed by a warm trickle down his left leg. The sun had risen above the hill and everywhere mist was burning off the earth, unfurling in great sheets toward the sky. The instant the sun struck her face, Yvonne turned to glance at it in the window. Sylvia leaned towards the mirror on her table. With the pad of her fingertip, she added a streak of lavender above each eye: — this, while the rats sought safety in the blackberry vines, in a huddle of warmth beneath some roots.

"It's time for breakfast, girls. Get out here."

Antone was alone on the hill, doomed to roam the bush, pursued by the barking of hounds. Squinting his eye at the sun, his face grizzled and torn, he felt the breath of the beast upon him: putrid, warm, and all-consuming. He willed himself to get down on all fours and to cock his head towards the sky, one ear awaiting instructions, wagging his phantom tail. Sylvia emerged from her bedroom, pirouetted across the kitchen floor.

"How do I look?"

Yvonne shot back, "Is beauty all you think about?"

"What's wrong with being beautiful?"

"Nothing. But alone, by itself, it's terribly insubstantial. Believe me."

Yvonne put the plates on the table and called for Michelle to come and eat.

"I'll be there in a minute."

"Not in a minute," Yvonne said. "Right now."

"I'm coming. I just have to finish something first."

Yvonne slid glasses of milk onto the table. "I'm going down to feed the animals. Have your breakfast eaten by the time I get back."

She shoved her feet into gumboots and went down the stairs to the basement. Pushing back the door, her nostrils pinched against the stench she expected to find on entering the dank cellar. But the smell of death had gone, like a vague memory. She filled a tin can with pellets, turned on the hose and headed down to the rabbit hutches. Vapor poured as though from a myriad of wounds hidden in the tall grass. She remembered the first time she had watched Antone skin a rabbit. He had cut the pelt free from around the head and tossed it, inside-out, onto the woodpile. Then he cut off the head and slit open the belly and plunged the whole of his large hand inside, pulling out a messy knot of viscera. She had felt carved out, as though someone had reached into her, relieving her of all desire, all life.

"Where's Mom?" Michelle said.

"Down feeding the animals."

Michelle climbed onto the stool at the end of the table and spread the picture next to her plate. "See the drawing I did for her."

"Nice," Sylvia said. "What's it supposed to be?"

"It started out being the cat, but it turned into a monster."

"What kind of monster has green eyes and a lavender face?"

Michelle shrugged. "I don't know."

"A frog with paint on it."

"Ha-ha. This isn't a frog. It's the monster I saw eating the sky."

"I'm sure Mom will like it."

Yvonne was in the garden pulling chard for the rabbits when she heard the lone howl rend the air. She stood absolutely still in the mist that rose around her, then suddenly she felt a tepid breath at the back of her neck, and shuddered.

Photo credit: Lise Macleod

ERNEST HEKKANEN

Ernest Hekkanen was born in Seattle, Washington, and moved to Canada in 1969. He currently lives in Vancouver, British Columbia.

Hekkanen has published stories, poems and prints in numerous periodicals, including *Canadian Fiction Magazine, Prism international, Malahat Review, Quarry, event, Descant, Waves,* and *Canadian Literature.* His work also appears in the anthology *Second Impressions* (Oberon, 1981). His first collection of short stories, *Medieval Hour in the Author's Mind,* was published by Thistledown Press in 1987.